Jennifer Johnston is recognised as one of Ireland's finest writers. Her other books include *The Gates*, *How Many Miles to Babylon?*, *Shadows on our Skin* (which was shortlisted for the Booker Prize in 1977), *The Old Jest* (winner of the 1979 Whitbread Award for Fiction), *The Christmas Tree*, *The Railway Station Man*, *Fool's Sanctuary*, *The Invisible Worm* (which was shortlisted for the *Sunday Express* Book of the Year in 1991), *The Illusionist* and most recently, *Two Moons* (also published in Review).

The Captains and the Kings

Jennifer Johnston

review

First published in Great Britain in 1972
by Hamish Hamilton

First published in this edition in 1998
by REVIEW

An imprint of Headline Book Publishing

10 9 8 7 6 5

ISBN 0 7472 5934 8

Typeset by Avon Dataset Ltd, Bidford-on-Avon, Warks

Printed and bound in Great Britain by
Clays Ltd, St Ives plc.

Headline Book Publishing
A division of Hodder Headline PLC
338 Euston Road
London NW1 3BH

To Ian

The two guards left the barracks at ten past four on the afternoon of September 20. The barracks, a small white house, was set in a terrace of similar houses, the only distinguishing features being a small sunburst over the door, signifying Garda Siochana, and a tall white flag pole on the roof for use on ceremonial occasions, which were very few and far between. They cycled slowly along the village street with the sun behind them and their shadows, black on the ground, always that unattainable length in front of them. Guard Devenney was the taller of the two men and the older and the least ambitious. For nearly twenty years he had lived in the village. His kids had been born and reared in the barracks and were all gone now, bar one. His wife had evolved from a tender girl, with soft nunlike white skin, into a woman of enormous proportions with a greying moustache fringing her upper lip. He knew everyone for miles around. He knew their weaknesses, he knew when to blink the eye. Guard Conroy was new to the job, new to the country, a Dublin man, with high hopes of quick promotion back to the hard, grey city streets again, where there was a bit of gas when you were off duty and the possibility of some real crime when you were on. The street curved sharply at the end of the village and their shadows moved round to the left-hand side.

'I don't like it at all,' said Devenney, more or less to himself.

Three children sitting on the edge of the pavement watched them go by without interest. There was no one else about. All indoors, no doubt, with nothing better to do but yak about what didn't concern them. Guard Conroy grunted in reply. He didn't believe in committing himself. Back at the other end of the village the level-crossing gates clattered shut behind the Dublin train. Smoke hung over the fields for a while, before melting.

'It's the sort of business goes sour on you. Heads fall. And I'll tell you one thing, it's never the Superintendent's head, nor the Inspector's neither.'

They rode on a while, in silence. The tyres of their regulation bikes crackled on the road.

'The law's the law,' said the younger man, for something to say.

'Ah, maybe. But trouble's trouble, just the same.'

It was hot for September, an Indian summer. The chestnut leaves were turning and the tops of the trees were gold against the clear turquoise sky. On the lower branches the leaves were still a tired green and the chestnuts hung in paler clusters, almost ready for dropping. It was the best part of a mile to the gates of Kill House and the two men were sweating by the time they arrived. They stopped outside the gates on the gravel sweep and each took a handkerchief from some interior pocket and wiped his face and neck. Guard Devenney even removed his cap and ran his handkerchief round the band inside before he put it back on his head.

'Well, here we go so.'

*   *   *

It was late May. The few remaining daffodils that fringed the avenue were turning brown and papery. The leaves were curling at the top. The early rose bushes in Clare's formal beds were covered in buds, which would begin to open with another couple of days' sun.

Since Nellie's death almost six months before, Mr Prendergast had taken to living more or less completely in the study. Books on the tables (where his father used to display his adequate collection of duelling pistols), on some chairs even and also in piles on the faded Chinese carpet. The piano sat in the middle of the room and in one corner there was a divan that he and Sean had carried from upstairs, in case of some unmentionable need. The two long windows faced south-west across the terrace at the wooded hills, and behind them the gaunt blue mountains constantly changed from one elusive colour to another. As the evening thickened, he would sit in his chair by the window and watch the green quivering lights spring up across the valley as people lit their lamps, and the moving fingers of light from cars on the main road below. It was almost his only pleasurable connection with the world. He would drink his first evening glass of whiskey as he watched and then, when he rose and crossed the room to switch on his own lights, he would refill his glass and settle down to read for the rest of the evening.

During the last few months of Clare's illness he had formed the habit of driving down to the church to play the organ. As the house became enclosed by the half light each evening, he had become obsessed by her eyes. For four months she had lain, propped up by pillows, in her bed, one side of her face pulled down into a sour little grin, her right arm useless, a cashmere shawl covering her thin shoulders. He would arrive in her room each afternoon as the clock on her mantelpiece chimed three and, picking up whatever book happened to be at hand, he would sit in the wing chair and read to her for an hour. The book was then closed and put away. He would move to the end of the bed and force himself to smile down at her.

'Anything you want, my dear?'

One eye stared coldly up at him, the other drooped as if in sleep.

'You're looking a little better today. Quite distinctly better. Have you up and about soon. Come the summer and you'll be out enjoying the garden again.'

He would bow and leave the room. He found it all most disconcerting, almost disagreeable. The memory of her eyes stayed with him until he left the house and drowned such thoughts in the vast chords of Bach.

He played the organ more often in the daytime now, as he found his eyes were giving him trouble in electric light. It was time he took himself to the oculist for new glasses but he preferred to live without them than make the journey to Dublin and back. From the moment of his marriage to Clare until his mother's death, his life had been spent in continuous movement. He had never stopped anywhere long enough to become accustomed to its rhythm. The moment a feeling of familiarity began to creep over him, or a new acquaintance seemed to have the audacity to be becoming a friend, then the trunks were packed, servants dismissed, tickets booked. They would move on. Clare's only pregnancy had been an irritating hiatus in his life. They had returned to sit it out with her family in North Oxford.

The atmosphere had affronted him. The roads upon roads of red brick, high-gabled houses, the smell of newly cut grass, the politesse over teacups, the indestructible goodwill of the English middle-class. After several weeks he had gone upstairs one afternoon and packed a suitcase.

'What are you doing?'

Clare had arrived home early from her daily walk.

'It should be obvious.'

'Are you going away?'

'Yes.'

He was embarrassed by the situation.

'I, ah, feel I'm wasting my time here. I thought I'd have a look at Sicily. Perhaps get in a few music festivals round the place.'

'You could go up to concerts in London from here.'

Her eyes dazzled with tears. He looked away from her, continued to pile neatly folded shirts one upon the other. 'I'm sorry, Clare. I can't stay here.'

'What will I say to mother? She'll think it's all most peculiar.'

'Say anything you like.'

Silently she watched him fasten his suitcase.

'You would have gone before I came home?'

He nodded.

'It would have been easier.'

'For you perhaps.'

'Quite.'

He picked up his case and leant forward to kiss her formally. 'Well, goodbye, my dear.'

She moved her head out of his reach. 'I don't understand.'

He ignored this. 'You'll be perfectly all right. After all, what could I do?'

* * *

After their daughter's birth they moved on again, leaving the child in the care of both her grandmothers. Neither lady had anything in common, apart from Sarah. Even this, they felt, wasn't a strong enough reason for them to become involved in the exhausting processes of communication, so the child shuttled between them, in the care of a good, old-fashioned nanny who knew her place and stood no nonsense, either from children, or interfering adults.

Her parents made it their business to visit Sarah at least once a year. They made responsible decisions about her education. They followed her scholastic career with interest and a certain amount of pride. She was a clever child. They sent her presents, not extravagant, for they were not flamboyant people, but interesting, sometimes beautiful, objects from every corner of the earth.

The war caught them in Mexico, where they stayed for a couple of years and then moved on to the United States. There they continued their nomadic life until the war was over. In 1946 they came cautiously back to Europe to find tired people desperately trying to build a new world. It seemed, at that time, as if it might be going to be a world in which there would be very little place for people like the Prendergasts.

One evening, as they sat in North Oxford surrounded by bleak post-war people and problems, ration books and a scarcity of domestics, a telegram arrived to say that the old lady was dead. She was being driven to dine with some friends by her man, Sean. Snow lay thinly on the higher hills and the roads between the black hedges sparkled with frost. Sean, exhilarated by a drop too much before setting out, drove just too fast on to an icy patch and the car went into a skid. They went off the left-hand side of the road into the ditch and hit a telegraph pole. Sean was unhurt but the old lady was dead. Her ringed hands were clasped, as usual, in her lap but her neck was broken. There was no sound anywhere but the humming of the telegraph wires and the drop of snow falling from the branches of the trees.

Surprisingly, they settled down. They didn't mix much; in fact, withdrew gently but firmly from the social ramifications created by the past. Clare and Sean had taken at once to each other and had thrown themselves, for their own different reasons, into the reshaping of the old lady's garden. Mr Prendergast took to reading. He wandered through books as he had wandered through the world, never quite grasping what it really was that he was looking for. He never read one at a time, always a pile were tumbled by his chair or bed. He roamed from author to author, century to century, prose, poetry, biography, essays, philosophy, history. He read, with fluency, books in French and struggled through German ones. Parcels arrived regularly from London and Dublin and he would tear the paper off like an impatient child and then carry the books into the study, where he would pick one of them at random, almost throw himself into a chair and start reading.

For pleasure, he played the piano. As a young man he had had reasonable talent but through the travelling years he had played little and his fingers had stiffened, and he played now with more than average skill but with caution.

Sarah intruded seldom. When her grandmother died she had

been in her last term at school. Her hair lay in two plaits on her grey uniform coat. Her face was like marble, white and still.

'So, you're off.'

Clare seemed to flutter in the hall behind him, like a moth in a cobweb.

'We haven't had much time for conversation. You've never told us why you've picked on Cambridge.'

'I thought it was time for a change of scene.' She wasted no words.

'We, ah, your mother and I have decided to stay on here for a while. At any rate. Straighten things up. We actually thought we might settle down here.'

'Oh.'

'You wouldn't think of . . . ?'

She shook her head. 'No. I think not.'

'Your mother, perhaps . . .'

Sarah looked briefly across his shoulder in her mother's direction. 'I think we'll all manage all right.' They kissed each other's cheeks. She went down the steps and got into the waiting taxi. The way she moved reminded him of his mother.

In order to keep the house alive old Mrs Prendergast had sold the land, hills, fields, bogland and wood to men who had been her husband's tenants and labourers. She watched with ironic eyes the golden and purple weed flowers creeping up through the corn as the years passed and barbed wire filling the gaps in walls. To keep himself and Clare alive, Mr Prendergast had closed the house room by room, floor by floor. Rows of unused keys hung on the wall by the kitchen door, under the coiled and silent bell springs. Only Nellie remained, indoors, and Sean, in the garden. After several years the book parcels dwindled and finally stopped altogether. Now he was alone and, it seemed to him, the way that he had always wanted to be.

Approaching nine o'clock and after his third glass of whiskey, the old man found his eyes sore and heavy and he threw his book down on the floor by his chair. He watched, for a moment, a furious fly beating himself against the window, bewildered by what seemed to be the sudden solidification of the air. He pushed himself out of the chair with a certain amount of trouble and went over to the piano. He sat pulling at his fingers, cracking the knuckles, trying to press the stiffness and swellings out of the joints. His head nodded as the fingers pressed. There was no point in looking for music. He would have to play what was in his head. He could hear it there, played to a perfection that he could never reach, or have reached, even before his fingers became so tired. The bell rang, a great jumping clatter of sound. He could see in his mind's eye the tarnished bell jumping on the end of its spring. Number one, the left-hand bell of the long, numbered line, high up on the damp wall below. Number two was the drawing room, three, the dining room, four, this room, father's study. There were only two things father had rung his bell for—turf and his boots. He had always refused to burn coal in this room and from September to May each morning the ashes were raked through and a neat pyramid built in the hearth. He could remember the fascination of watching the dry turves catch and the timid first flames crawling up the inside of the structure.

The bell clattered again and, whoever the unexpected guest might be, he was banging now with the huge iron knocker. The old man got up slowly and crossed the room. Sometimes, now, in the evenings, if he moved too fast or incautiously, cramp knotted the muscles in his calves so inextricably that he had to sit, motionless, in his chair for up to half-an-hour. 'Coming, coming,' he muttered irritably in reply to the hammering. 'Coming.'

He opened the door and found a boy on the step. As far as the old man was concerned he could have been any age between a large seven and an under-nourished, under-privileged seventeen. Tight coiled springs of orange hair covered his head.

'No need to batter the door down.'

The eyes that peered up at him were honey-coloured, secretive. The face pale, already fatigued by living.

'Who might you be?'

The boy didn't answer. He pulled a white envelope out of his pocket and offered it.

'Hey?' Mr Prendergast ignored the letter. 'Can't you speak?'

The boy stared down at his black shoes, which looked as if they had been contorted into their particularly alarming shape by a hundred pairs of feet.

'For heaven's sake, boy, I'm not going to eat you! Hey? I don't often eat boys. Never Celts. They're stringy.' He looked down at the outstretched hand, the bitten nails, the envelope. 'I joke,' he muttered to the air.

It was almost dark and he knew that the last rays of the sun now painted the chimney stacks away above their heads. The air was sweet and moist.

'Look at me, hey, boy.' The boy looked up. 'You know my name?' The boy nodded. 'What is it, then? Let me hear you say it.'

'Mr Prendergast, sir.'

'Splendid. That's the first hurdle over. At least I know you're not a deaf mute. Now, tell me your name.'

'Diarmid, sir.'

'A splendid name.' The boy's mouth stretched slightly in a smile. 'An historical name. Tell me, Diarmid, what do you know about the Diarmids that have gone before? If anything, hey?'

'I don't know, sir.'

'You don't know what?'

'I don't suppose I know anything much.'

'That's honest, anyway. There's many a man goes to the grave without admitting as much.'

'I'm not too keen on school, like. I don't go much . . . I mean . . . you wouldn't let on?'

'I wouldn't. What do you do when you're not at school?'

For the first time the boy really smiled. 'I keep out of the way, sir.'

'A wise precaution.'

They both looked at each other, weighing up carefully what they saw.

'Come in,' ordered the old man. 'There's a rising mist.' He stood back and let the boy pass him. Then he closed the remaining light out. The hall was large and very dark now, like a cave. 'Straight across. I presume you have another name.'

'No, just Diarmid.'

'A tribal name, at least. You must belong to someone.'

They came into the study and the old man groped on the wall for the light switch. Illuminated, he stood, his head shaking slightly, looking at the boy with a mixture of interest and embarrassment, wondering why he had invited him in. 'Diarmid . . . ?' he asked.

The boy was staring round the room. Outside, a gold pencil

line divided the black sky from the black earth. In a moment that, too, would disappear.

'Oh, Toorish. It's like a shop in here. Are all these things yours?'

'Mine? Yes, yes, they're mine all right. I take it you're connected with my late housekeeper in some way. Miss Nellie Toorish.'

'Yes,' said the boy vaguely, still trying to come to grips with the room. Suddenly he remembered the letter and held it out once more towards the old man. 'This,' he said.

'Ah, yes. Thank you.'

Mr Prendergast took the letter and inspected the writing on the envelope, leaving the boy free to edge round the room touching things, picking up a book, a dusty Meissen figure, a photograph, examining them with fingers and eyes. It was only when he came to the piano and touched the bottom note that the old man reacted.

'Ah, no,' he said. 'The hands must be clean. Otherwise the notes become grimy, unpleasant to touch. Come.' The boy stood by the piano, listening to the fading growl of A. 'Diarmid Toorish. This way.'

He spoke sharply. The boy followed him out of the room and down the passage to the kitchen. The old man filled the sink with hot water, placed the Sunlight soap to hand and fetched a towel from behind the door.

'There.' He pointed to the sink and then to the boy's hands, just in case any mistake might be made. 'Wash.'

Mr Prendergast opened the letter while Diarmid washed his hands and then dried them on the towel, leaving long grey streaks as he rubbed. The old man waved the half-read letter in his direction. 'So Nellie was your aunt.'

The boy nodded and began edging towards the door.

'I'm surprised she never taught you the importance of clean hands.' He hung the towel up on the back of the door again, looped over a printed overall that had been Nellie's and a greasy Burberry that had been there for ever, unworn, unclaimed. This had been the flower room before circumstances had made it necessary to close up the basement. A glass door led out on to the flight of stone steps that arched over the area and down on to a sanded path.

'I never seen much of her. She didn't get along with Mam.'

'She had a strong personality.'

The boy wasn't interested. He held his hands up in front of the old man's face and perked his head in the direction of the other room. 'May I . . . ?'

'Run along.'

The words were neatly placed on grey lines, each loop meticulous, each bar neither too long nor too short.

Dear Sir,

begging your pardon for troubling you. My husband, J Toorish Groceries ltd, is the brother of the late Miss Nellie Toorish, RIP, as you will know, and we wondered if you would have a place for the boy in the garden, as he must leave school come June, being then almost fifteen. He can read and write, but much more for him I cannot say as he hasn't spent much time on his studies. He has no great wish to go into the shop, but I'm sure he'd learn the gardening easily. One thing to be said for him is he's honest.

yours truly

Kathleen Toorish (Mrs)

※   ※   ※

In the study the boy was touching the piano notes, singly at first, then in discordant combinations.

'Ah,' said the old man with irritation. He folded the letter and put it into his pocket. As he entered the room, the boy looked up and smiled.

'No, no, no, boy. You go and sit down. Anywhere. I'll play something for you. It must please the ear. Make yourself at home. Just a minute.' He went over to the window and picked up the whiskey bottle from beside his chair. He looked vaguely round for glasses. 'In the kitchen, by the sink.'

They both stood looking at each other.

'Well, jump to it.'

'But what, sir?'

'Glasses, for heaven's sake, boy. Upside down, draining. And some water.'

Diarmid moved.

'A jug . . .'

'I'll find something, sir.'

'For God's sake stop calling me sir,' muttered the old man, unscrewing the top of the bottle. The need for a drink suddenly became so great that he quickly took a short, guilty swallow. The boy came back, balancing three glasses, one filled with water.

'I couldn't see a jug handy.'

'Splendid. A fellow of initiative. Here, just a little for you. Fill it up with water. When I was your age I was a veteran drinker. My father believed in teaching a man to hold his drink.'

'My father's a pioneer.'

'Poor, misguided fellow . . . The trouble with us, as I see it—

Celts in general, I mean—is that we tend to exaggerate. We exaggerate the limits of both liberality and frugality. Other examples spring to mind.' He looked at the boy's blank face and waved him to a chair. 'Sit down, boy, whatsit. I'll play you something. Then we'll discuss your mother's letter. I suppose.'

He shut his eyes to play and visualized the notes of a Nocturne rising and falling on the empty page of his mind. The boy sat in the chair by the window holding carefully in his hands, as if it were alive, the faded, brown silk tassel on one end of the silk rope that tied the curtain back.

'Frederic Chopin,' said the old man, turning round from the piano, 'born in 1810. He was a Pole. Poland is a country with a history not unlike our own. Tragic and violent. I don't know when he died but it's immaterial. He was comparatively young. How do you like your drink?'

'I don't mind it.'

'And the music?'

'I didn't mind that either.'

'Well.' He got up slowly. Every joint ached if treated roughly. 'To business. I suppose you know what is in your mother's letter.' He took it out of his pocket and waved it round in the air for a moment.

'No.'

'Your mother thinks it would be a good idea if you came and worked in my garden.'

Diarmid looked up at him, totally surprised. 'Garden?'

'Mmmm. I suppose they think that Sean can teach you something. Misguided. Sean is . . . well . . .'

'Barking.'

'Well, I suppose you could put it like that. Only when the

15

spirit moves him. Spirits, I should say. That's beside the point. I haven't the money to pay another hand.'

'I don't want to be a gardener.'

'Well, that seems to sort out that problem.' He poured himself another drink.

'I always thought I'd like to be a soldier. I suppose they wouldn't take me yet a while.'

'I think you're possibly a little young.'

'I thought the British army.'

The old man was suddenly tired of the whole thing. 'I think it's time you went home. High time you were in bed.'

Reluctantly the boy got up. He swallowed the last drains of the coloured water and looked around the room, trying to find some reasonable excuse for staying. A glass-topped table caught his eye. He moved towards it.

'Are those medals?'

'They are. Let me see now . . .' He felt in his pocket and found a two-shilling piece. 'Here. I'll write a note to your mother in the morning. Don't feel up to it now. You come up sometime tomorrow and collect it.'

The boy paid no attention to the coin. 'Yes. I'll do that. You can tell me about the medals then. OK?'

'I suppose so.' He put the money back into his pocket and brought the boy to the hall door.

* * *

The old man had forgotten his visitor by the time he reached his bedroom door. Until Clare had become ill they had shared, for traditional if no other reasons, the large room that had been his parents', the master bedroom, with the western view out over the valley. Then he had moved, without regret, into a smaller room at the end of the passage and had never bothered to move himself back. Through the window you caught glimpses, beyond the elms, of a lake created by his grandfather. No one had bothered with it for years and the patch of water was slowly being crushed by weeds and rushes. Soon there would be no echo of the sky, fair or foul, to be seen amongst the green.

Sometimes, on the landing, his feet would automatically carry him to the door of what he now thought of as Clare's room. Only the feel of the cold, unused handle in his palm would remind him and he would turn away. Clare's body had shrivelled on the bed until it had become impossible for life to continue any longer. In the last few weeks of her life her body had hardly crushed the pillow or creased the sheets. He had never touched her then, never taken her hand or bent to kiss her grey cheek. Nellie had lifted her like a baby, had insisted on sharing, with the nurse they had had to call in towards the end, all the personal chores that he preferred not to know about. When Clare finally died, Nellie had nearly gone mad with grief. She had apparently believed, for some reason the old man couldn't grasp, that this humiliating state of suspended animation was better than death.

He had felt a sense of huge relief, as if a rock that had been tied to his back had suddenly been removed. He had taken his walking stick and gone striding down the avenue to the village where he had sent a telegram to Sarah. 'Your mother died this morning. Father.' He handed the form across the counter to the post-mistress and she counted the words in silence. She made several cryptic signs on the form and then put the pen down. She blessed herself. 'God rest her soul.'

'Amen.'

'Four and six. You could have phoned it and saved yourself a walk.'

He laid a half-crown and a florin down on the counter.

'It's Nellie would miss her, I'd say.'

She crooked her hand around the money and swept it into the cash drawer. 'A sad day.'

'Yes.'

He was hypnotized by the blueness of her eyes through her glasses. What more could she want? Why would she not let him go?

'A nasty shock a telegram like that would give you.'

'She's been expecting it for some time,' he excused himself.

'Just the same, a mother's a mother.'

'Yes. Well . . .'

'I'm sure you've a lot to do. Arrangements . . .' she dismissed him, recognizing his inability to come up to scratch.

He left the post office feeling that he should have come out of the conversation better.

He slept little, three hours at the most. Some nights he was almost certain that he never slept at all. Inside his head pictures came and went, snatches of conversation or music, faces he found the greatest difficulty, if he succeeded at all, in putting names to. It was all like turning over the pages of some friend's photograph album. Here were people he believed he had never given a second thought to, places that had left him cold, irritatingly crowding out of the dark crevices of his mind and causing him irritation because they insisted on being labelled. When the effort to remember became too great he would sit up and switch on the light and read until the words, merging and unmerging in front of his inflamed eyes, became meaningless marks on the page and he would doze off, his head slumped on his chest, his mouth ungainly open. Discomfort would wake him and the process would start again. Now, though, he was no longer angered, as younger people are, by the evasiveness of sleep, merely resigned.

The morning after Diarmid's visit Mr Prendergast got up early and put clean sheets on his bed. He folded the old ones carefully and put them into a pillow case, along with four shirts and three pairs of underpants. Sean would take them away with him when he was going and bring them back clean in a few days. Outside, the lake was hidden by a grey mist being drawn up from the grass by the early morning sun. Tea and toast was all he ever had for breakfast. As he ate it he read the *Irish Times*, which a boy from the village dropped through the letter box every morning at seven thirty. The tin teapot he left bubbling on the stove as Sean, if he came, always needed a good strong mug to clear his head. If there was no sign of his arrival before the old man had finished the paper, he would know that the gardener was having one of his bad days and he would empty the mess of glutinous leaves into the bucket. This day, though, Sean banged on the door just as Mr Prendergast was folding the paper into a suitable shape for reading the leader columns. He continued to fold and, after a moment, the irritable banging was repeated. He propped the paper against the milk bottle and went and unlocked the door.

' 'Morning, Sean.' He sat down again and, leaning forward to focus, began to read.

'Sir,' was Sean's contribution.

The gardener looked as if he should have been a jockey, small and bow-legged, with a brown check cap that never came off except, presumably, if and when he went to bed. What could be seen of his face was red and swollen from exposure to the weather and alcohol. Sometimes the flesh round his eyes swelled up to such an extent that it seemed impossible for him to see through the slits that were left to him. His mug was waiting by the stove. He poured himself the full of it and stirred in three spoons of sugar. He carried around with him, like a travelling salesman carries a suitcase, a smell of alcohol and general decay. As it reached Mr Prendergast he took out a handkerchief and banged at his nose impatiently, as if his nose was inventing the smell.

Sean sucked a mouthful of tea in and held it in his mouth for twenty seconds or so before letting it slip noisily down his gullet. 'It's great old weather,' he said, 'great, so it is.' The old man unfolded the paper and cast his eyes over the letters to the editor. 'A couple a days a this and them roses will be bursting out.' He sighed dramatically. 'God rest her soul.' He repeated the tea-drinking operation. 'I hear that young fella a Toorishes was up here.'

The old man put the paper down on the table. 'Yes.'

The two men looked at each other.

'Well?'

'Well, what?'

'What did you say to him?'

'I see. You know. You are perhaps . . .'

'I just heard,' said the gardener sourly.

'It's out of the question.'

The gardener looked a shade brighter. 'I wouldn't trust him as far as I could throw him. That's just personal, mind you.' He scratched at a cheek with his brown horny nails.

'I appreciate that. You should realize better than anyone else how impossible, impossible . . .' he emphasised the word by banging on the table with his knuckles '. . . out of the question. You know what I mean. Financially.'

'That's all right, then,' said the gardener, rinsing his mug out under the tap and leaving it upside down on the draining board. 'I'll be off so. There's a pile to do at this time of year.' He went out, leaving behind him for a while his strange, unwanted smell.

Dear Mrs Toorish,
I regret that I am unable to help you by giving employment to your son. In the past, as you no doubt recall, we had gardeners and under-gardeners in abundance. Now, alas, times have changed and it is as much as I can manage to pay Sean Brady the few pounds that I do. I also feel, in all fairness to your son, who seems, on a very short acquaintance, far from stupid, that you should discuss with him any plans you may be making for his future.

I remain, etc etc formalities and so on.

He re-read it and grimaced. Most of it was irrelevant but, just the same, he folded it and pushed it into an envelope. It would surely give offence, he felt, licking the flap, put a quick stop to anyone else around thinking that maybe he was a charitable organization. He put the envelope on the mantelpiece, propped against what he had always considered to be an excessively vulgar Dresden parrot, to await Diarmid's return.

* * *

The bell jangled just as Mr Prendergast and Sean were finishing their lunch. Many years before Clare had decided that Sean, if he were not provided with one hot meal a day, would all too soon rot the inside walls of his stomach with too much undiluted alcohol and she would be without a gardener and ally. So Nellie, much against her will, had been ordered not only to provide him with a meal but to make sure that he ate it. Nellie, being someone to whom all the intricacies of social distinction were an open book, pursed her lips and said nothing but did as she was told. Since her death the old man had continued with the routine and he and the gardener sat in almost total silence, one at each end of the kitchen table, and ate in rotation the three different dishes that circumstances had forced Mr Prendergast to teach himself to cook. For all the interest either of them took, he might have saved himself a lot of trouble and merely taught himself one.

The bell rang.

Mr Prendergast turned over a page. The book flat on the table by his plate was *Sodome et Gomorrhe, Part One*. He preferred to read it in French as, in spite of the perfection of Scott Moncrieff's translation, he preferred to interpet the subtleties of Proust's prose for himself. Across the table Sean chewed as he stared out of the window. At first, in self-protection, the old man had offered him books and newspapers but the gardener had brusquely shaken his head without saying a word. It was only then that he remembered how Clare had sighed, years before, over the fact that Sean couldn't read. She had toyed momentarily with the grand idea of teaching him but the gardener hadn't the will to learn nor she the drive to teach. His own comments at the time he could no longer remember but he was sure they had been effectively demoralizing. Each day, as he placed the book

carefully by his plate, taking care not to damage the spine as he
flattened the pages, he would look across the table at the
gardener. 'If you'll excuse me . . .'

'Fire ahead,' Sean would say.

'It's the bell.' Sean leant across the table towards his employer
who had heard nothing. Nose always stuck in a book, he
thought with contempt, or banging away at that old piano.
No time for a soul. Hardly a civil word out of him in the
course of a day. 'Mawnin', Sean, Evenin', Sean,' in his bloody
West British accent. Not like herself at all. There was a real
lady, even if she was English. Never a cross word, always kind,
even during his bad moments. And he'd been in a queer bad
way when they came first, owing to—well, best not thought
of owing to what. That's when the head starts, when the eyes
get tight and hot and the sound of humming wires grows and
grows, filling the whole body. She took him in hand, right
from the start, never a cross word, even in the winter when the
day came round, never a frown, she knew what he was going
through. Put his hand in the fire if she asked, only to ask and
he would. 'It's the bell,' he repeated. 'I wonder who that would
be now?'

The old man, disturbed by the sound of his words, looked
up. He focused his eyes with difficulty. 'What's that?'

'No one calls here.'

'Thank God.'

'It's the bell.'

The bell jumped and twisted on its spring.

'Well, well,' said the old man, closing his book. 'I suppose
you wouldn't like to go and see . . .'

'I'm the gardener,' refused Sean, reasonably.

'Quite.' Mr Prendergast got up and went to open the hall door.

Diarmid let go of the bell. 'You told me to come back.'

'Have you never heard of patience? I seem to remember yesterday also you . . .' He indicated the bell with his hand. 'We . . . ah . . . surely had words on the subject then. Hey, boy, what?'

'Right you be, sir. A nod's as good as a wink. Next time I'll stand outside and whistle. Here. Looka. I washed my hands this time.'

He held his hands up above his head, the startling pinkness of the palms towards the old man. He peered at them and nodded. 'You'd better come in.'

He stepped aside and the boy went past him through the door and straight across the hall to the study. At the door he turned and jerked his head, asking permission to go into the room.

'Go ahead. If you don't mind amusing yourself for a few minutes, I'll just go and finish my lunch.'

When he went back into the kitchen Sean was rinsing his plate under the tap, scratching the congealed food into the sink with a cracked nail. Mr Prendergast sat down and opened his book once more. Shining drops splashed off the plate and scattered on to the floor.

'Leave it, leave it, Sean. I'll do that.' He always had to do it, anyway. There was always this farce. Sean banged the plate down on to the draining board, wiped his polluted finger on his trouser leg, adjusted his cap, paused for a moment in his journey across the room to see if the old man would tell him who had been at the door, and then marched out and down the steps. Mr

Prendergast watched his ungainly progress.

The treads of the steps were so narrow that the normal foot, even when placed sideways on them, overflowed dangerously. He watched how the sand from the path scattered out from under the heavy feet, some of it on to the edges of the grass, which was ragged with uncared-for springtime growth. He was heading for the potting shed where he would have a little smoke, probably a little drink, possibly a little sleep, at any rate strengthen himself for an afternoon's work out in the weather.

While the kettle was on the boil, the old man tidied up the kitchen, rewashing Sean's plate with his own, drying them carefully and putting them away. Then, reaching down two cups, he made some Nescafé and carried it into the study.

Diarmid had opened the display table and was standing by the window with a medal in his hand. As he heard the old man come into the room he asked, without turning round: 'Is this yours?'

Mr Prendergast crossed the room and looked over his shoulder. The boy had square hands with short, thick fingers and badly bitten nails. The knuckles were swollen and scarred from winter chilblains. Hands of an unmitigated plainness but they held the medal with enormous care.

'No. That one was my grandfather's. A noble fighting man. The Crimea, I think that was. Yes. That's right.'

'Oh.' The voice was slightly disappointed.

'Ever heard of the Crimea?'

'No.'

'Tttt. What do they teach children in schools these days?'

'It's like I told you. I don't go much to school.' He threw his head back and laughed loudly. 'Maybe they're all learning about the Crimee, or whatever you said, this very minute. I doubt it, though. They never teach you anything interesting. What did he do?'

'Who?'

'The fella got this.'

'I've no idea. Killed a hundred Russians with his bare hands, no doubt. He was rather a flamboyant gentleman.'

'Flamboyant?'

Mr Prendergast put down the coffee cups and took a miniature from the table. He held it out for the boy to look at. 'Here.'

Tiny diamonds glittered round the frame.

'They don't wear clothes like that now.'

'It's probably just as well, they'd be a bit conspicuous on the battlefield. The whole technique of war has changed since then.'

'I could see myself in that.'

'Shot dead by a long distance marksman with a telescopic lens. Drink up your coffee before it gets cold.'

'But what sort of thing would you have to do? That's what I'd like to know.' He transferred his attention back to the medal again.

'A moment,' said the old man. He went over to the bookshelves and peered at a row of peeling spines. 'Drink it up,' he repeated rather irritably.

The boy paid no attention.

He took down a copy of Tennyson and blew along the top. Dust drifted away like a wisp of smoke. 'Listen to me, now. This is what you want to know.' The skin on his hands was almost as dry and transparent as the rustling pages. He stood by the fireplace and began to read.

Half a league, half a league,
Half a league onward,
All in the valley of death . . .

The boy stared out across the terrace at his own valley. On the higher slopes the golden flame of the gorse was spreading through the stone-spattered fields. When he was quite sure that the old man had finished, he moved over to the table and carefully put the medal back where it came from. 'Volleyed and thundered . . .' he whispered.

'Well—? What did you think of that? Isn't that what you were after?'

'Which of them is yours?' Diarmid looked down at the relics.

Mr Prendergast put the book down and went over. They looked like tombstones lying there on uncared-for green velvet grass.

He touched a cross with one finger. 'That one?'

'Yes.'

The metal was cold, made, he felt, from the cold metal that killed. 'I never knew you were a soldier.'

'A temporary fit of madness. A situation arose when it was impossible . . . a lot of people died. It was to have been the war to end all wars.'

'Were you very brave? What did you do?'

The old man picked up the cross and put it into the boy's hand. 'I was young. When you're young you think you'll never die. It makes you act in a reckless way. Even when everything around . . . everyone . . . Some people call it lack of imagination, others, courage.'

'You must have done something.' The boy's voice was impatient.

'I survived. That, I suppose, is worth commemorating with a bit of decorated metal.'

'You're a terrible old cod.'

There was a moment's rather frightening silence and then the old man began to laugh.

'An old cod. That's a good one. Nobody's ever called me that before.'

Weakened by his first laughter in years, he groped for the sofa and sat down. The room seemed to tremble with alarm. The boy, embarrassed by his own words, turned over the cross in his hand and stared at the back of it. The laughter came in short jerks. Mr Prendergast clutched at his chest; the unaccustomed exercise was causing him a certain amount of pain. Discomfort, as they would insist on calling it nowadays.

'You have a point. That's just about what I am.'

'I'm sorry,' muttered the boy without looking up. 'It just slipped out. You made me mad by being so . . .' he thought for a moment '. . . fancy. I like to understand.' He smiled suddenly, looking directly into the old man's face. 'Cannons to right of them, cannons to left of them volleyed and thundered . . . I understand that OK.'

Mr Prendergast leaned back against a cushion. His head was throbbing and his heart seemed to be pulsing in a space that was far too small for it. 'I am too old for laughter.'

Diarmid picked up the nearest cup of coffee and carried it over to him. 'Here.'

'Thank you, boy.' He straightened himself with effort and took a mouthful. It was pretty disgusting and barely luke. Much better to drink tea, really, than this ersatz rubbish that always made you slightly queasy as it plunged into the digestive system.

Before, Smiths of the Green had posted a pound of Continental Roast beans once a fortnight and Nellie had ground them, as the need arose, in a green, box-like grinder with a brass handle. As she turned the handle, the house was always filled with the friendly smell of coffee beans. Now there seemed little point. He noticed, as he put his cup down, the boy's fingers caressing the surface of the medal. 'Put it away,' he ordered abruptly. 'It's not something I really care to be reminded about.'

The boy nodded. He put the cross away and shut the top of the case. 'It's a great gadget, that. For putting things in. Like a museum. I went to a museum once, and I up in Dublin with my auntie. They had cases like this all over the place. A lot of coins and things like that. Do you find coins interesting?'

'I can't say I do.'

'She didn't want to stay long. It was only because it was raining we went in at all.'

'Perhaps you'll go again some day.'

'I never liked my auntie.'

It was the time of the day the old man usually spent sleeping. About an hour he slept, sitting in the high-backed chair by the window, his head dropped on his chest, his mouth fallen open, so that when he woke his neck was always stiff and his mouth was filled with a taste of stale air. He could now feel his eyes becoming heavy. A yawn arose inside him. It was well past his accustomed time. He waved a hand towards the mantelpiece. 'The letter for your mother. You'll find it up there.'

'No bother yet a while,' said the boy. 'I can't go home just yet. Amn't I meant to be at school?'

'I must sleep. Old age . . .' he began, almost apologetically.

Diarmid smiled. 'I won't bother you.'

'I don't know what I should say.'

'I wouldn't bother saying anything.'

'Save my breath, hey?'

'That's right.'

Surprisingly, the old man went asleep.

He slept about his statutory hour. He lifted his head with difficulty and stared at the pearl-like strings of cloud moving slowly across the sky, then at the boy in his chair, his head bent in concentration over the copy of Tennyson. He looked up as the old man moved.

'You've slept a long time. It's near on four. I'll have to be going soon.' He shut the book.

'Don't you expect to be discovered some day?'

'There's not much they can do. Only hit me. I'm used to that.' He grinned for a moment. 'My father hasn't a very strong arm.'

'The so-called authorities tend to have stronger arms than parents.'

'Ah, who cares.' He put the book on top of a pile that the old man had left beside the chair at some time or other. 'So, if you'll give me the letter for Mam, I'll be getting along.'

'Of course.' Mr Prendergast got up slowly.

The boy watched, his face wrinkling up with the old man's effort. 'I'd hate to be old.'

'Some people think it's better than being dead. There's no alternative.'

'What do you think?'

Mr Prendergast took the letter from the mantelpiece. He stood looking at it for a moment. The all-enveloping, unconquerable shakes were creeping over him again. 'I'm pretty tired these days.'

'Tired of being alive?'

'I think, rather, tired by being alive.'

The boy came over and took the letter from the trembling hand. 'You could always do away with yourself.'

'The idea doesn't actually appeal to me.'

'Sammy Ryan hanged himself the other week. My friend saw him just after they'd cut him down. His face was black. He was a bit wanting. Mam said it was a mortal sin.'

'I think I'll take my chance with the rest.'

'What did you say in the letter?'

'That is between myself and your parents. If they see fit . . .'

'They. She, more like. He can't even switch on the TV without her allowing him. "Morris, do this; Morris, do that. Morris, fetch in the coal, wouldya. Morris, don't put your shoes on the covers. Morris, wouldya punish the child. Morris . . ." Ah, hell.' His eyes were hard golden stones.

'Well, I think . . .'

'Last evening when I got home she was in the front room. Her head was bulging with big iron curlers.' He waved his hands around his head descriptively. 'You always know Thursday. Curlers. Ready for confession on Fridays. "Where were ya? What kept ya? What did the old fella (that's you) say?" '

'I really don't want . . .'

Nothing was going to stop the boy. His body had become possessed by the metal-headed fury. The old man resigned himself.

' "If he said nothing what kept you so long? The piana. Nellie said he was always banging on that, true enough. No, you can't watch TV. Get on up to bed, I'm sick of the sight of you.'" He came to himself once more and looked apologetically at Mr Prendergast. 'It's like that,' he said.

'We all have our problems.'

'I'd better go.'

'Yes.'

'Can I come and see you another day?'

'I suppose, if you want to . . .'

'It won't be over the weekend. They make me work in the shop on Saturdays, and Sunday's there's Mass and I have to stay at home after that because my Granny comes.'

'Run along home, boy. I've had enough for one day.'

Weary of conversation, Mr Prendergast sat down at the piano, clenching and unclenching his hands to try and make them fit for playing. The boy let himself out without another word.

Once out of sight of the windows of the house he stopped and, taking his penknife from his pocket, he carefully opened the letter and read what was inside. It was not a difficult operation, he had done it many times before.

✳   ✳   ✳

Friday was the night for choir practice. Mr Prendergast pulled himself together with a strong drink before going round to the yard and getting out the car. The windscreen was yellow with age. He took his handkerchief from his pocket and rubbed the glass in front of the steering wheel. It made very little difference. Sean's bicycle leant against the yard wall still, but there was no sign of the gardener himself. Mr Prendergast backed carefully out of the garage and turned in the yard. The cobbles were covered with a fine coating of moss. The window of what had been the harness room had been without glass for many years. The evening ground mist was filtering its way between the tumbledown buildings. The old man hadn't noticed desolation since his settling in.

It only took a couple of minutes to get to the church but these last few months he had preferred to drive. He felt less vulnerable, as if he were not really leaving the house at all. The rhododendrons were purple and white and crimson, massive flowers with stamens held out expectantly. They sickened him. One day, he had always threatened, he'd have them all burnt down, rooted out. The inevitability of nature disgusted him, the ever-turning wheel. Clare had always been emotionally moved by it, had made idiotic breathless remarks in springtime. He thought suddenly that a surprising thing had happened during the course of their lives together. At the end he had known less about her than he had thought he had known in the beginning. Things had got lost on the journey, rather like the odd suitcases, or rugs, his father's racing glasses, all things that had mysteriously disappeared in the course of their travelling.

He turned sharply in at the church gate, scraping the front mudguard along the granite wall. 'Damn.' At the vestry door he got out and looked at the long white scrape on the paint. Little glitters of mica lay on the wound. 'Damn.'

The Rector materialized beside him, like some rather unpleasant spirit in his cassock which, much to the old man's disapproval, he had taken to wearing in the street. Ridiculously flamboyant, almost verging on High. Mother would have spoken strongly. She had taken a very strong stand when some Rector with advanced ideas had changed from The Church Hymnal to A and M, or was it vice versa? Whichever it had been, mother had adamantly refused to move with the times and all members of her house who attended the Church of Ireland took their hymn books from the hall table each Sunday and would spend most of the service fluttering through the gold-edged pages trying desperately to find the words they were supposed to be singing. The old lady herself never opened her mouth in church, except to speak, with great clarity, the expected responses. She would pray with her gloved hands placed palm to palm, like a Botticelli angel, and her pale face lifted slightly heavenward.

'Well, well, well, old man. Damaging church property?'

'I think, rather, that church property's damaged my car.'

'Took the corner a trifle sharp, I fear.'

'Mmm.'

'No great damage done, though.' The Rector inclined, rather than leant, towards the mudguard. 'One's eyes start playing up as one gets on.'

'My eyes are perfectly all right.' He had all his life lied to James Evers.

The Rector put his hand on the old man's shoulder and drew him towards the church. 'We wouldn't like to lose our organist.'

Mr Prendergast wrenched his shoulder free from the Rector's grip. 'If you'll excuse me, I came early to put in a little bit of practice.'

His footsteps echoed in the empty church. The Rector stood by the door watching as he settled himself at the organ, switched the light on, rubbed at his fingers for a moment. He shut his eyes so that he couldn't see the watching figure. Pretentious blithering fool, in his fancy dress. Incompetent shepherd of a dwindling flock. Ten on a good day. His hands reached out and the first notes of a fugue touched the unused air. Son of a local Bishop, always asked to nursery tea and then later to tennis. Not enough gumption to do anything but follow in father's footsteps.

Never yet managed to preach a decent sermon. Too ironic to come back and find James established here, of all places. Clare had talked gardening with them and done the expected good deeds. Chatted over teacups. All dross. Why torment yourself with face to face confrontations? Why try to communicate? This terrible post-war urge. Everything that had to be said was there, on the bookshelves, dancing on the staves, on canvas. Find your own salvation there. If that was what you felt the urge to do.

Eileen Evers clattered in to the music. She came at him from behind and leaned her tissue paper cheek against his. She smelt faintly of witch hazel. He took his hands from the keys.

'Charles, dear.' She straightened up, the salutation over.

He turned towards her and smiled with civility. Every Friday evening it was the same. They eyed each other like boxers.

'We must get together and have a good chat sometime soon.'

He smiled thinly in reply.

'Why don't you come back with us this evening and have a bite? Pot luck. Please do. James would be so pleased.'

The old man lifted his hands in a helpless gesture. 'I must decline.'

'Nonsense, Charles.' Her voice had become slightly shrill and domineering. 'Why must you decline? You become more and more ridiculous every day. Of course you'll come.'

Silently he shook his head.

'We worry about you.'

'I assure you there's no need.'

'After all, you are one of James's oldest friends. And, of course, dear Clare.' She sighed.

'Absolutely none whatsoever. How many times do I have to say it?'

The door at the other end of the church creaked and voices could be heard. Mr Prendergast reached for the hymnal with relief. Mrs Evers, with a charming smile, turned to meet her husband's parishioners.

The Rector himself came out of the vestry and switched on the lights in the choir. Some narcissi at the foot of the pulpit, that had looked and smelt so sweet last Sunday, drooped pitifully. The old man played a few experimental chords and then folded his hands in his lap and waited until the choir was ready to begin.

'And how is dear Sarah? What's the news from London these days?' The Rector spoke to him in the porch as he was hurrying out. Down the other end of the village the bell of the Catholic church struck nine times. Automatically the Rector took his watch from his pocket and looked at it. He adjusted the minute hand a fraction. 'Irritating.' He put the watch back where it had come from. His Christian hands were long and pale against his cassock. Fragile with age. They could have been the hands of a musician, thought the old man, if only the old fool had had anything stirring in his head.

'I hear from Sarah very seldom. She leads a very busy life.'

'Surely a visit from her is overdue?'

'It's not much fun for her over here. She doesn't really know anyone. There's, ah, not much to do. Young people like . . .'

'It's her home.'

The old man looked startled for a moment at the severity of the Rector's voice. 'Oh, no,' he said. 'It's never been that.'

'Well, you know what I mean.'

'She'll come if she wants to.'

'Why don't you drop her a line?'

They had reached Mr Prendergast's car. He opened the door. 'I think she's as well off where she is.' He hesitated, not quite liking to get into the car with the Rector still fluttering beside him. 'I like to be alone.' He said it as an explanation, not a rebuke.

The Rector pursed his lips and shook his head slightly. 'Of late, my old friend, you have become, how shall I put it . . . ?'

'Put it how you like. I am old, James. We are both old. We have a right to behave as we wish. No longer to be bound by . . . ah . . . conventions.'

'But friendship?'

'Think clearly, Rector. At no time in our lives has there been friendship between us.' He got into the car and groped for the key in a panic. The engine began to vibrate. He reached out and closed the door between the Rector and himself. The white, Christian hands hung limp, like the dead flowers at the foot of the pulpit. Behind him the windows flushed and flamed, reflecting the western sky. He edged the car gently forward.

Eileen came out of the porch and stood beside her husband. He spoke some quiet words to her out of the corner of his mouth. She raised her hand, cheerfully high, and waved to Mr Prendergast.

I'd better be careful, he thought as he approached the gate; another bump and they'll have my licence removed.

*   *   *

It was several days before Diarmid turned up again. The door stood open and he walked in without waiting for a yes or no. He dawdled his way through the hall. A grandfather clock that had stopped a few days after Nellie's death caught his fancy. He opened the case door and set the pendulum swinging. The figures on the face were brass and the ornate hands pointed permanently to twenty-five past three. There was a sound from the kitchen. Quickly he shut the clock. The pendulum moved slower without his helping hand. He went on down the passage to the kitchen.

The two men sat at the table, Mr Prendergast behind the paper, Sean, unprotected, chewing with great care. His teeth gave him trouble. They seemed to have shrunk in their sockets and sometimes it felt dangerous to eat. He looked over at the boy as he came in. The old man put the paper down on the floor.

'Well, well, well.'

'Hello.'

'Would you look what the wind blew in,' said Sean disagreeably.

Diarmid ignored him. 'I've brought you this.' Carefully he took from his pocket a large, luminous-looking duck egg. The shell was patterned like the moon's surface with ridges and bumps. He held it out towards Mr Prendergast.

'Well . . .' repeated the old man.

'Who'dya pinch that from?' Sean mopped round his plate with a piece of sliced loaf.

Mr Prendergast took the egg gingerly into his hand. It had a smear of mud or excrement on it.

'A duck egg.'

'Not a duck or a hen, if it comes to that, to be seen around your back yard, anyroad,' commented Sean through the bread and gravy.

'It's a present.'

'So I gather. I am most touched and grateful. I used to be

very partial to ducks' eggs. It's been a long time. Thank you, boy, hey.'

'Scallawag. It's a good larrup on the backside you need, not thanks.' Sean got up and carried his plate over to the sink. He dropped it in with a clatter.

'Never mind him.'

'Oh him; sure, why would I mind him?'

'You steal one flower out of my garden and you'll mind me. Or go bringing your friends up and galloping over the place. Let me warn you. Here and now.'

His eyes were really bad today, the old man thought; sunk right back into his head, rimmed with moist red. He must be coming up for one of his turns. As if the old man's thought had reached him the gardener groaned slightly, a disconcerting noise, and then took from his pocket a handkerchief of sorts and wiped, most carefully, one red slit and then the other. He examined the handkerchief with interest and groaned again before returning it to his pocket.

Diarmid paid no attention to the groans. 'You're not the boss around here, anyway.'

' "Mind the garden, Sean," the mistress said with her dying breath,' lied the gardener.

The boy looked unimpressed.

Mr Prendergast put the egg down carefully on a saucer. 'I think we've had enough.'

'And mind it I will, 'till I drop in me tracks and there's some that appreciate what others do for them and some that don't.'

'Oh, I do. I couldn't have managed without you.'

The gardener smiled fiercely in the general direction of Diarmid, pulled his cap down over the sad, red, slits of eyes and went out into the garden. They watched him go down the steps in silence.

'He has turns. His life hasn't been all it might have been. You mustn't pay too much attention to him.'

'He's an old sod. I don't know how you stick him round the place.'

'Ah, well yes,' said the old man. 'How long . . . ?'

'I had in mind to stay till school was over. If it's all the same to you.'

'I have no plans.'

'Will I put the kettle on for coffee so?'

'That would be very kind.' He began to clear the table. 'What was your mother's reaction to my letter?'

'She said nothing to me at all but I heard her say to me Dad, "I might have saved the ink."' He lit the gas. 'They're in a right way, now. They don't know what to do with me at all.'

'They must be worried.'

'Worried in case they can't get rid of me. They think if they have me in the shop I'll be getting into trouble, dipping my hand in the till, adding up the bills wrong, eating and not earning.'

'I think you exaggerate.'

'They say as much to my face. My father should know the ropes, anyway. Doesn't he nick the petty cash himself a half a dozen times a day. She keeps him very short, I suppose he's not to be blamed.'

'And you?'

'Huh?'

He had to stand on his toes to reach the Nescafé tin which was on a shelf above the stove.

'You. Would you, ah, be carrying on like that?'

'I don't steal money.'

'Just things like duck eggs?' suggested the old man.

'Where will I find a spoon?'

Mr Prendergast handed him one out of the basin. The boy dried it carefully before measuring the powder into each cup.

'I'll take it back if you don't want it.'

'Oh, no. I didn't mean that. I was only making a dirty crack.' He looked at the boy frowning, as he worked the coffee and a little milk together with the spoon.

'You look like a little old man, frowning away there.'

The boy looked up at him and smiled. 'And you're behaving like a little boy, making dirty cracks.'

They both laughed.

'I only pinch things because I like them. Not because I need them. Isn't that all right?'

Mr Prendergast reached for the whiskey bottle and poured a small tot into each cup. 'It improves the taste. I refuse to make pronouncements on the rights and wrongs of stealing.' He put the bottle away and took a large bunch of keys from a hook near the door. He peered at the labels. The writing on some of them was so faded that it was impossible to read more than a letter here and there.

The kettle boiled and Diarmid filled the cups with water. The smell of warm whiskey rose with the steam.

'Bring the cups, boy. I've something to show you.'

The first flight of stairs had tarnished brass rods holding the carpet in place. Nellie used, once a week, to slide each one out from its slots and polish it golden and for a while the hall and stairway would smell of Brasso. She sang always as she did this job. Sometimes now, as the old man climbed the stairs, her voice came into his head. 'Come back to Erin, mavourneen, mavourneen. Come back, machree, to the land of your birth . . .' The cloth would squeak as she rubbed it up and down the rod and the smell of the polish flew up your nose and made you sneeze if you happened to be passing.

The top flight had only tacks which held the remaining rags of carpet to the floor. Up at the top, the long passage between the locked doors was lit by two half-moon windows, one at each end of the passage, perfectly symmetrical. Long creeper fronds tapped against them now, incessantly, impatiently, wanting in . . . The light in the passage was constant twilight. The smell was musty and all the time the tiny noises made by unused rooms brushed your ears. The end room on the right had been the nursery. Three windows to the south-west caught the afternoon sunlight in tangles of spiders' webs. Everywhere that dust could lie was filmed with grey. The chairs were sheeted. A large grey bear with one eye stared down from the top of a cupboard.

'It was the nursery. The playroom,' he explained, seeing the boy look puzzled. 'Look.' He opened a cupboard. Inside on the dusty shelves, neatly stacked as if only yesterday some creaking, crackling nanny had tidied them away, were boxes of soldiers and equipment. Each box was carefully labelled, spidery thin-nib, black writing, starting to fade now after many years. Black Watch, Lancers, Gurkhas, Field Artillery, Red Cross, Foot Guards, Dragoons, Légionnaires. Miscellaneous. 'My brother and I were great collectors.'

The boy moved to the cupboard and opened one of the boxes. He stared, fascinated, at the soldiers.

'We were very proud of them. Mind you, they're a bit out of date now. It must be almost sixty years.' He nodded to himself and whispered quietly '. . . or more'.

Diarmid was lining some men up along the edge of a shelf.

'. . . More. A bit more than sixty years since the last ones were bought. He was older than I.'

'What was his name?' He didn't sound really interested. He opened another box.

'Alexander. After my father.' The boy picked out a galloping horseman. 'That's an Uhlan. Ever heard of them?'

'No.'

'A very famous German regiment. There's a book downstairs. It will tell you all about them. We'll have a look later.'

'Thanks. Where is he now?'

'Who?'

'Alexander. He must be very old. Or is he . . . ?' He paused discreetly.

'He's gone a long time ago.'

'Gone?'

'1915.'

'Oh.' He began to root in another box.

'I was on leave when we heard. It was in the summer. Nobody liked opening telegrams in those days. I was here, so we knew . . .'

'Knew what?'

'Knew it was he.'

'It might have been something else.'

'It never was.'

Mother and Father had been out, somewhere, couldn't recall, irrelevant, anyway, and the telegram had lain on a silver salver in the hall for several hours. He had gone to his room and lain, waiting, on his bed. Alexander's voice sang in his head—'Röslein, röslein, röslein rot, röslein auf der heiden . . .' And as he heard the car door slam and his mother's laughter on the steps, the singing stopped. He ran down the passage to the bathroom and vomited into the basin.

'Your hands are shaking.'

'I must sit down a minute. It's . . . the stairs.'

The boy pulled the dust sheet off the nearest chair. A grey cloud rose into the air. Imperceptibly it settled again, this time also on the intruders. Mr Prendergast lowered himself into the chair. He clasped his shaking hands between his knees in the hope that the pressure would force the convulsive movements to stop. No thought of Alexander had entered his head for years and now it was as if the young man was there, inside his mind, tearing down walls expertly built by time.

'Wer reitet so spät durch Nacht und Wind? Es ist der Vater mit seinem Kind . . .' As the walls fell, the song grew louder. The old man's fingers trembled now for the piano. He had never mastered the accompaniment then.

'No, no, boy.'

'I'm sorry. I'll try again.'

'You must practise. I keep telling you.'

'I do. But when you sing, it eludes me. Listen, I can do it.' He played a few phrases.

'It won't do. Honestly, Chas, it's terrible. Mother'll have to play.'

'Alec . . .'

'Not a word. Mother.'

When Mother moved it sounded as if someone was unwrapping a parcel of tissue paper. She came in from the garden at Alexander's call. She always came at Alexander's call.

'Well? What is it?'

'You must play for me. He is impossible.'

She swept Charles off the piano stool with a hand. 'You must practise more, my darling.' She sat down in his place and quickly began pulling her rings off and clattering them into a porcelain bowl on a table nearby, as if they were worthless pebbles. When her hands were bare she opened and closed her fingers several times and smiled up at her son. The old man felt the burn of jealousy in his stomach and remembered the smell of burning leaves that drifted past him as he stepped out of the window into the cool evening.

'It must have been autumn.'

'What?' Diarmid was staring up at him from the floor, where he was sitting surrounded by boxes.

'I'm sorry. I was very far away.'

'Sometimes I think you're a bit gone, you know.' He examined each man with care before putting it on the ground. 'I never seen soldiers as good as these before.'

'They don't make them like that nowadays. There's a shop in London that would give you a lot of money for these, in fact. If you go over to that cupboard by the window you'll find a book called . . . *Famous Battles* . . . something like that. It's full of maps and plans. We . . . he and I used to recreate them . . .' he gestured with his still shaking hands. 'All the floor was our battlefield. We used to take it in turns to have the winning army.'

'That would be a great idea.'

'Somewhere there's a box full of generals, field marshals. Even, if I remember aright, Le Petit Caporal himself.'

'Who's he when he's at home?'

'One of the greatest generals of all time. A rogue, mind you. A villain, rather. Alexander, Caesar and Napoleon Bonaparte. If you hand me down that box up there in the corner, I'll show you.'

The boy put the box on the old man's knee. He sat down on the floor again and watched Mr Prendergast's hands carefully as he picked his way through the great men of war.

'Yes, indeed, I suppose these probably have a considerable value nowadays. The Lord Protector. I'd forgotten we had him.' He held him out, warts and all, in his fingers towards the boy. 'Alexander had great admiration for Cromwell. It was one of the many subjects on which we differed.'

'Is that Cromwell? Can I see?'

'I thought that name might strike a chord in your peasant skull.' He handed Cromwell over to the boy.

'He was an ugly-looking git, anyway. Why did your brother like him?'

'He liked efficiency and order. He thought that perfection could only be achieved through discipline.'

The boy thought about that. 'I suppose that's what's in the back of their minds when they larrup you at school.'

'I doubt it, boy. I doubt if much is in their heads at all.'

'I'd laugh to see Mr Moyne's face if he heard you say that.'

'There. That's Napoleon.' The Emperor stood, feet slightly apart, the hand stuck between the coat buttons, shoulders hunched, his peasant face brooding, in the palm of the old man's hand. 'He was a giant.'

The boy looked startled. 'A giant?'

'Metaphorically. A giant among men. He ruled almost all of Europe until one day he went too far.'

'What happened?'

'As a general, he overstretched his lines. As a man, he misjudged the character of his enemy. They were desperate and cunning. They lured him deeper and deeper into Russia, stretching his lines to the limits. They knew that, inevitably, Nature would be on their side. He thought he'd won the prize and then, literally overnight, they broke him. They say he got into his coach in Moscow and didn't get out until he reached Paris. That's romancing, of course. But he was lucky. Thousands and thousands never saw France again, let alone Paris.'

'Was that the end of him?'

'The beginning of the end. He was a hard man to finish off. Beaten in the end by an English army with an Irish general . . . a bit of help from the Germans.' He peered into the box. 'I don't recall that we had him.'

'And if he hadn't gone to Moscow, he'd have gone on ruling almost all of Europe?'

'I don't suppose so, really. It was just a matter of time. With time every tyrant's thinking becomes clouded. Had he thought more clearly he might have conquered Ireland, but he was preoccupied with things he thought were more important.'

'I might be a general.'

'You never can tell. It's an advantage to have been to school from time to time. Acquire some knowledge. It always comes in handy.'

'I can read, can't I? I can teach myself. What I want to know, not just what they decide they want me to know.'

'Unfortunately, we don't necessarily know what we need to know until it's too late. Like I said, if Napoleon had known more about the Russians, he'd never have gone all the way to Moscow. Into the trap.'

Diarmid took Napoleon from the old man and examined him closely. 'One thing I do know, anyway, is not to stretch my lines too far.' The old man laughed. 'I don't think much of his uniform.'

'He was never a flamboyant dresser.'

'That man downstairs, in the picture, was he a general?'

'No, alas. Merely a flamboyant dresser.'

'Flamboyant.' He tasted the word in his mouth, like a new piece of food.

'Peacocks,' suggested the old man.

The boy put Napoleon carefully on the shelf, not on the floor with the commonalty. 'I'll have a look at them all first and then, tell you what, we'll have smashing wars. Like you and he did.' He went back to the boxes.

Mr Prendergast watched him for a while then fell asleep, a sleep without dreams, without alarms. When he awakened, Diarmid was standing on a chair replacing some boxes on the top shelf. His face, hands and adolescent wrists were caught in the gilding sunshine. Benvenuto, thought the old man. Pure rascal.

'You snored,' said the boy.

'My wife always used to say so.'

'If my wife snores, I'll kick her out of bed. The noise coming out of Mam and Dada's room would waken the dead.' He stepped down from the chair. The old man saw that his face was streaked with dust.

'You're filthy, boy. What's the time? You'd better wash before you go home or your mother'll wonder what you've been up to.'

'Tomorrow will you show me that book?'

'What book is that?'

'The one about battles.'

'I suppose so.'

'I might come up a bit earlier.' The old man started to push himself up from the chair. 'You wouldn't mind, would you? Here, let me give you a hand.'

'I can manage, boy. I am not totally incapacitated yet. Though no doubt my time will come.'

'But would you mind?'

'What time you come? That's entirely up to you.'

'I could do a few things for you.'

'I don't think that . . .'

'Around the place, like.'

'It's very kind of you . . .'

'There's always things to do.'

The boy looked at Mr Prendergast and laughed as he watched him straighten himself carefully.

'We all grow old,' said the old man, with reasonable good humour.

'I won't.'

'Permit me to laugh this time.'

'What happened to him?' The boy nodded his head towards Napoleon. 'Did he die a hero's death?'

'No.'

'Oh.' The boy was taken aback.

'He was exiled. He spent the last six years of his life a prisoner.'

'He could have killed himself.'

'He could. You seem obsessed with the idea of people killing themselves. It is, as you know, a mortal sin.'

'It's always there for you to do. If you don't like the sort of life you have to live. Have to.'

'Your life is supposed to be in the holy hands of God, for Him to do what He likes with it. You are not supposed to take these decisions for yourself.'

'What's the time?'

The old man took his watch from his pocket. 'Getting on for five.'

'Mother of God, I'll be murdered. She'll ask me questions.' He put his hands over his ears, as if to protect them from the battery of shrill words.

'What'll you say?' He gave the boy a gentle shove towards the door.

'I'll think of something. I'm a great hand at inventing.'

They walked along the passage. A fly buzzed somewhere, caught irrevocably in a spider's web.

* * *

'I got kept in, Ma. I'm sorry I'm late.'

'Your tea's ruined. What were you up to this time? Nothing ordinary, I'll be bound.'

'It was spelling, Ma. I hadn't . . . I'd forgotten me stint.'

'The same old story. Wait till your father hears you were in trouble again and he'll give you what for.'

* * *

There was a distinct smell of mice, the old man thought. Perhaps a cat. But what, in the end of all, did it matter if the mice took over. When he was a child the passage had smelt of beeswax and friar's balsam. Both he and Alexander had been chesty and small lamps filled with friar's balsam had burned in their rooms during the winter. Somehow, even though the windows were wide open all through the summer months, the heavy smell had always lingered in the passage. He wondered why he had stayed on in this white elephant of a place after Clare's death. He should have taken something more compact, more suitable to his way of living. Sarah, at the time, had suggested that he move to London but the idea hadn't appealed to him. Didn't appeal to him now, either. Nor did the idea of the tentative and probably painful gestures that would have to be made if he and his daughter were to create even the most formal relationship.

'I think, in fact, I'd be safer to say I went along the river with Mick and never looked at the time. Mick is my friend, only I'd never trust him with my life.'

'Can you swim?' asked the old man.

They stood on the steps. There was a little breeze which lifted Diarmid's hair gently from his forehead and let it fall again. The rooks were having their afternoon fling and the sky seemed full of their ungainly bodies.

'I've never tried. We just fish a bit and throw stones. Skim, you know, if we can.' He skimmed an imaginary stone across the grass and through a rose bed.

'We used to swim in the lake.' He nodded over beyond the trees. 'In the summer we used to spend nearly all day down there. We had a boat and we used to take all our clothes off and dive in from it.'

The boy looked him up and down. The old man realized with embarrassment that he was trying to visualize what he must look like naked.

'A long time ago,' he said, in the direction of the rooks. 'We were boys.' Diarmid nodded. 'If I got Sean to cut the rushes back a bit in places, you and your friends could use it, if you wanted. With the summer coming on.'

'That would be great. I'll cut the rushes, though. I'd like to do that, if you want them cut.'

'I can always get Sean . . .'

'I'd like to.'

'You'll need a sickle.'

'I'll get one of them all right.'

'I'm sure if we asked Sean . . .'

'I wouldn't ask that git for anything if he was the last person left on earth.' He held out his hand. 'I've had a great afternoon.'

Formally and awkwardly they shook hands. Diarmid, with a wave of both arms, leapt down the five steps at once and ran down the avenue. At the bend he turned and waved again but the old man had gone into the house and closed the door. The boy whipped across the grass, bending low as he ran. He took his penknife from his pocket and cut three newly opened rose buds. The outside petals were brilliant red and the hearts were yellow. As he went on down the avenue he examined them closely. Their smell was very sweet.

'Flamboyant,' he whispered and put them carefully inside his jacket.

✻ ✻ ✻

'That one is here again.'

It was already eleven thirty and Sean had only just arrived. He had brought the groceries from the village and left them on the kitchen table. Hearing the sound of the piano, he had put his head round the study door to announce this piece of information.

'I thought you weren't coming.'

'I'm not feeling too good.'

You could smell the drink from him. Each time he moved the smell intensified and then faded slightly until the next gesture. His clothes must have steeped all night in whiskey, thought the old man. He got up from the piano.

'Do you want a cup of tea?'

'I didn't like to let you down.'

'I appreciate that. I do, indeed.'

'I couldn't keep tea down.'

'Coffee, perhaps?'

'Nothing.' The humming of the wires always started gently but it inevitably filled his head with a sound that nothing could drown, not even alcohol. 'Couldn't bloody keep anything down at all.'

The old man looked out of the window. The haze that had covered the valley in the early morning had almost completely lifted and everything dazzled in the sun.

'We're really in for a heat-wave.' The gardener only grunted. His head was splitting. 'Well, if you won't have a cup of something . . .'

'Amn't I after telling you, that one is here again.'

'Who?'

'That Toorish boy. I seen him nipping through the rosiedandrons and I coming up the avenue.'

Mr Prendergast sighed. 'Just leave him, Sean. He'll do no harm.'

'I'm sorry I interfered.' He withdrew, his face sick and angry.

By lunchtime he would be in a black mood and round about five he would grope his way from side to side down the avenue and along the road to his hovel, that was the only possible name for it, and that would be the last time that anyone would see of him for up to a week. Sometimes it had even been two weeks and he would come back thin and crazy-looking, his hands shaking so much that he was hardly able to lift the fork to his mouth. Nellie had always raged on and on at him as he sat there opposite her, desperately trying to eat, for the sake of peace, but the old man left him alone to recover his equilibrium as best he could.

Mr Prendergast took his blackthorn stick from the hall stand and went outside. It was safer to take it these days if he intended walking any distance at all. He walked slowly down the avenue and branched off along the path through the rhododendrons that led to the lake.

Diarmid had taken his trousers off and thrown them on the grass. He was standing up to his waist in water attacking the rushes. The sickle flashed like the sun on the water as it rose and fell.

'Good morning, boy.'

The boy looked up at him. 'It's muddy.'

'Always been like that round the edge. It's clear further out. Aren't you cold?'

'No. Look what I found.'

He moved slowly along the bank. Under the streaks of mud the old man could see that his legs were white, like they'd never before seen the light of day. He threw the sickle on to the grass and, stooping, gently pulled aside the rushes and uncovered a nest with three eggs in it.

'A moorhen,' said the old man.

'She went squawking away as if the devil was after her.' He laughed. 'Right enough, I near chopped the head off her.'

'She'll be back.'

The boy covered the nest again then climbed out of the water on to the grass. He shook like a dog and a thousand drops of shining water whirled away from him.

'Are you stopping?'

'Jaysus, no. I've only started.'

'You can have some lunch later, if you like. I doubt if Sean'll be wanting any today, so there'll be a chop going begging.'

'Great.'

Above them a lark's voice rose and fell in unphrased song. The old man looked pointlessly up to see if he could catch sight of the bird. He was many years too late.

'Like I said, I can't swim, though.' He bent down to poke some mud from between his toes.

'That's a bore.' Somehow he'd thought that all boys could swim. Everywhere he'd ever been, water had always seemed full of swimming children. He couldn't remember a time when he hadn't been able to swim. 'Old motorcar tyres are a help.'

'Yeah. That's a great idea all right.' He picked up the sickle and slithered into the water again. 'Give me a shout when you want me up at the house. I'll carry on with this. It's a job you could be for ever doing.'

'Herculean. Don't overdo things, Hercules.'

He was glad of his stick on the way back to the house. He was constantly irritated by his increasing lack of mobility, by the discomfort he suffered in his bones. He was frightened, not of death, which now was so inevitable that it was like waiting for a visitor who never told the time of his arrival but you knew was on his way; rather, by the thought that one day he would be unable to get out of his bed and would be forced to lie, like Clare had done, wasting away. Imprisoned. He struck angrily at the grass with his stick. If he could strike the ground open and be swallowed, how splendid. No debris. Alexander had been hit by a shell. Very little debris there. Miscellaneous fragments, not worth gathering up. Mother had insisted that an empty coffin be buried with full pomp, here, in the churchyard. She had sent him packing the next day, unable to bear the sight of him. She had looked at him, he remembered, as if she'd thought that somehow it was his fault. Even a year later she still wore black. It was a colour that had always suited her. After the war was over, uniform in moth-balls, neatly folded into the black tin trunk in the attic, he had left home. 'A travelling man.' He'd once heard one of the maids describe him thus. 'Though I am old from wandering through hollow lands and hilly lands . . .' It didn't apply. He had merely been routed, weakling that he was, by a lady in black, whose diamonds flashed with grey splendour each time she moved her hands. The mica in the granite steps flashed ferociously up at him, baiting him. He wondered what Sarah had done with the rings. Clare had never worn them. Her hands had been too . . . no, it was her personality that had been colourless. She had been too retiring to control such jewels. They would have overpowered her. They had lain in their boxes until after her death. He had taken them from their velvet boxes and laid them all on the table in front of Sarah. She picked one up and slipped it on to her finger. In his head his mother's laughter glittered like the stones.

'It's not me. I'll never wear them.'

'Take them, anyway. They're yours. Sell them if you want to.

What good are they doing anyone shut up in a drawer? Hey? You may have children.'

Sarah laughed shrilly. The sound set his teeth tingling.

'That's unlikely.' She took the ring off and put it back in its box. 'But if you really want me to have them . . .'

'I never want to see them again.'

Had he said that, he wondered, or merely thought it?

A horn blew. He stopped on the top step and turned round to see who was arriving. A small green car, being driven with extreme caution, came round the bend. It was too late to take cover. The Rector's hand moved in blessing or salute. The car, narrowly missing the bottom step, stopped in a series of diminishing jumps. It coughed. The Rector stared at his hands for a few moments, as if he were surprised to see them side by side on the steering wheel. He was wearing a grey flannel jacket. His TCD scarf hung limply around his collared neck. He had left his cassock somewhere else. He got out of the car and coughed like an echo. 'Ah-ha . . .'

'There's not much in it as far as bad driving is concerned.'

'We're not getting any younger, my friend.'

'Are you coming in?'

'If I may.'

He climbed up towards the door, his spindle legs buckling under him slightly as he moved from step to step. In the hall he peered round, worried, judging.

'I live as I live,' said the old man shutting the door. 'I'll make you some coffee if you like.'

'Thank you, Charles, that would be most acceptable.'

They moved in silence towards the kitchen. The shopping that Sean had brought earlier still lay on the table. The old man put the kettle on before beginning to clear away the groceries.

'You manage?'

'I manage.'

'We worry about you, Eileen and I.' He sat down and folded his hands in his lap, as if he were about to start praying.

'I had hoped that I made my position clear to Eileen the other evening.' He put two cups without saucers down on the table. The Nescafé tin was already there. He measured a heaped spoonful into each. 'I apologize for this. I find real coffee too much of a problem.'

'We drink this all the time,' said the Rector gloomily. 'I don't find it agrees with me at all.'

'If you put a little of this in it takes the harm out.' He reached up to the shelf for the whiskey. 'Will you join me?' He could see by the Rector's face what was turning over in his mind, what he would be saying to worried Eileen during dinner that evening.

'I? No, thanks. Ah, hum. You know how women are once they get an idea into their heads. If I've told her once, I've told her a thousand times there was no need for worry. If anyone can manage on his own, I said, it's Charles. But she insisted, nonetheless.'

The kettle boiled. Mr Prendergast made the coffee. Let him get on with his own mission. He'll get no polite help from me. The Rector moved his hands in a strange nervous gesture and then reclasped them.

'I pray for you.'

'Oh.' He was disconcerted. 'I suppose I should say thank you.' He pushed the coffee and the sugar across the table.

The Rector stared into the swirling brown liquid with distaste, though whether it was for the situation he was in or the coffee it would be hard to say. 'You don't have to.'

'Well, I will. Thank you.' He poured a goodish measure of whiskey into his cup.

'No matter what you say, I've always considered us to be good friends—no!' He unclasped his hands quickly and held one of them up, like a policeman in white gloves, at a crossroads. 'You were about to speak.'

'Yes. I . . .'

'Don't, I beg of you. No more unconsidered, splenetic words. I know you value your solitude. I appreciate . . . sometimes, indeed, I have envied . . . yes. But we would feel so happy if you would visit us from time to time. There is so much behind us and, in this world, so little left. We would value it . . . Old friends become rare as . . .'

'Oh, very well,' said the old man, trying hard not to sound too splenetic. 'I'll come and visit you from time to time.'

The Rector looked relieved. He lifted up the cup and took a scalding sip. 'Capital.' He smiled triumphantly across the table. 'Eileen will be so pleased. Why don't you come back with me now and have a spot of lunch. Pot luck.'

'I regret. I am already committed.'

The Rector's face lost its smile. 'I don't want to press you.' His words were like cold stones of hail beating on a winter face.

In the distance the door opened and shut. The Rector, mouth pursed with disapproval, raised his cup once more. The old man, moving at his own top speed, went to the kitchen door and down the passage to the hall. Diarmid stood quite still by the door, half alarmed. He was still wearing only his shirt and held his trousers, socks and shoes in front of himself self-consciously. He jerked his head towards the door and the car outside.

'Upstairs, third on the right. You'll find a towel in the hot press.'

Without a word, the boy ran across the hall and up the stairs, leaving a trail of mud and drips behind him. The old man returned to the Rector with a slight smile.

'My lunch guest.'

'I'd better be off.'

'There's no rush. Though I'm sure you've other calls to make. In the, ah, course of your parochial duties.'

The Rector stood up. He pushed the half-finished coffee across the table. 'Nothing is as it used to be.'

'It's called evolution.'

James Evers brushed the remark aside impatiently with a flutter of his fingers. 'When I was a young man the Church was the backbone – no, more than that – the nerve centre of a healthy society.'

'That's how you saw it. A narrow view, if I may say so.'

'We never saw eye to eye.'

'Precisely.' They moved slowly out of the kitchen.

'And you'll come and see us,' pressured the Rector once more. 'Drop in. Have a drink or something, if you won't come for a meal. A chat with Eileen. She gets perturbed.'

'No need.'

The Rector looked down at the floor. 'Your guest was very wet.'

'Mmm.'

He waited on the steps until the car had disappeared.

* * *

The sun marched majestically through the rest of May and the first couple of weeks of June. Clare's roses had never been better. Each morning as Diarmid passed through the garden he cut an armful and the hall and the study smelt sweet and reminiscent of youth.

Sean didn't reappear for ten days and then he spent most of the day shivering in the potting shed, hiding from the sun. He seldom spoke but if his eye lit on Diarmid his face became stiff with hate.

The boy cut back the rushes at the edge of the lake until there was a wide channel through which he would push a tyre out into the middle, where his feet couldn't touch the bottom. He would splash around out there for half an hour or more. As the days passed his naked body turned from white to pink and then, gradually, a very pale brown.

Sometimes the old man would put on his panama hat and take his stick and walk slowly down to the lake. He would lower himself gracelessly on to the grass and sit there reading until his back became insupportably sore; then he would, with Diarmid's help, get himself to his feet and go slowly back to the house again. Sometimes he played the piano or sat by the open window reading or sleeping and would suddenly find that Diarmid had silently arrived and was sitting near him, motionless in the golden light. He almost always brought a present when he came. Another duck egg or two thick slices of rich fruit cake, a slab of yellow butter with the imprint of a flower on it and tiny salty beads of sweat lying on top. Once a music manuscript book; another time a honeycomb. Mr Prendergast asked no questions, accepted with a smile and shared, when possible, the gifts. The main part of their time, though, was spent up in the nursery, the floor covered with soldiers, maps and books. There they observed military formalities, saluted each other and addressed each other with military titles.

In the evenings, after the boy had gone and the heat and brilliant light were draining away from the garden and the growing fields as the tide patterns its way out across acres of wet sand, the old man sat by the window, his drink by him on the floor, and realized the beauty of peace.

As June continued clouds began to trouble the sky and black shadows passed from time to time over the house and garden. A sharp wind rippled the water of the lake and made bathing little pleasure. The boy became daily more remote, withdrawing into unhappy thoughts of his own.

'What's bothering you, eh, boy?' The old man sat at the piano. The words had been in his mind for a long time. The boy moved uneasily in his chair, squirming like a fish that didn't like the taste of the hook. 'Hey?' Mr Prendergast turned round and looked at him, demanding an answer.

'They're going to send me away.'

'Away?'

'I listen at doors. I read their letters. I know they're conniving. Is it terrible to do those things?'

'It's certainly socially unacceptable. Maybe you have misinterpreted things.'

'Got things wrong?'

'That's it.'

'No. I'm not an eejit.'

'I'm aware of that. Where are they intending to send you? A school somewhere?'

'Not on your nellie. To Dublin. They're looking for a good job for me in a shop up there.'

'You're very young. Are you sure?'

'I have this auntie.'

'Ah, yes. The lady of the museum.' He turned to the piano and very softly played the first phrases of a fugue with his right hand.

' "Mary can take him for a year or so. 'Till he's old enough to fend for himself." ' Mrs Toorish's voice minced into the room. ' "After all, she's little enough else to do. She'll be glad of the extra coming in each week. Whatever, anyway, he'll have to go out of this, we can't have him idling around here another minute. He'll never come to anything at all if we don't get him out of here soon." '

'Honour thy father and thy mother that thy days may be long in the land which the Lord thy God giveth thee.'

'That's the Bible.'

'Exodus twenty, twelve. It was quoted constantly to us in our youth.' The left hand came striding in. 'You're very young,' repeated the old man, over the music.

'You keep saying that.'

'When I was your age . . . what does that matter. When I was your age, indeed.'

He concentrated on the music for a while. Chords swelled and faded. The walls seemed saturated with the sound. The boy put out his hand and held the old man's shoulder gently. He could feel through his fingers the movement of the bone in its socket, the movement of the music. When the fugue was finished they were silent for a moment.

'Yes,' said the boy. He put his hand back into his pocket. The old man turned and looked at him.

'You've all your life in front of you. Dublin's as good a

place to begin life as any. Better than most, probably.' He nodded, thinking aloud. 'I've travelled the world over, boy, and I can't think of a better place to start from.'

'You didn't start as apprentice to a grocer.'

'True.'

'Anyway, I didn't think much of Dublin when I was there before. It's maybe changed since your day. Nor my auntie.'

'Maybe you've got it all wrong. They'll have to discuss it with you.'

'Divil a bit of discussing. "Tomorrow your Dada's taking you to Dublin and I'll have no lip out of you. If you don't like it you can lump it." And the next day she'll hand me the case and shove me out the door with him and that'll be that. I bet she won't even come to the station and wave . . .'

The old man got up and went over to the window. He stared out at nothing, but out of the side of his eye he watched the boy fidgeting restlessly with a button on his jacket.

'I enjoyed the train ride. There and back. I came back on my own. A lady bought me a cup of tea in the restaurant car.'

'That must have been nice.'

'It was OK. You need money to be a traveller.'

'I certainly got through quite a bit. But there are those who can make a profit out of it.'

'I want to be a soldier.'

'It seems to me it's all just a question of getting through the next few years until you're old enough to enlist.'

Sean appeared on the path below the windows with his wheelbarrow and started scuffling weeds with a regular rhythm, developed over the years to use the least effort. Scratch, scratch, the blade pushed the weeds in small heaps in front of him on the gravel. He didn't look up at the window.

The boy ducked down behind the big chair, his fingers touching the ground, stooped as if he were about to begin a race.

'What are you doing? What on earth . . . ?' Diarmid poked his finger towards the window. 'Foolishness. Utter.'

But the boy stayed where he was, relaxed a little, down on to his knees, a finger traced the faded complications of the carpet. 'They catch you before you can do anything about it and put you in a cage.' He looked up at the old man. 'That's what it looks like to me, anyway.'

'What a strange child you are. In all the best stories the hero runs away.' He regretted it the moment he had said it but Diarmid didn't seem to be listening. 'You could almost say that I had run away and where did it get me?' He put his hands out wide to embrace the room.

'So, you're off?'

A sod of turf slipped in the edifice and sparks chased each other up into the blackness of the chimney. Mother reached out from her chair and rang the bell. The diamonds and the sparks became confused in the blackness of his mind. Her hand returned to her lap and lay motionless beside its partner. Father, older than his years, was crumpled upon the sofa. His face, devoured by the years, hid a mind that had almost ceased to function. *The Pilgrim's Progress* lay open on his knees, as if he had just laid it down for a moment; in reality he carried the book round with him from room to room, chair to chair, all through the long day, without it occurring to him to read a page or even a few lines.

'Yes. The car is waiting.'

She sighed. Her hair was still golden, a halo round her unsaintlike face. 'You will never make anything of your life.'

He bowed slightly towards her. 'Thank you for a mother's blessing.'

She laughed, throwing her head right back against the chair, almost joyfully. Father moved on the sofa and muttered something under his breath.

'He,' she said, when the laughter stopped.

'Yes, yes. I know what you're going to say.'

A maid came in and went over to the fireplace. In the afternoon they wore dresses of dark brown stuff, with pale coffee-coloured aprons. She knelt down and began to rebuild the fire. Mother and son watched in silence. The girl rose after a few moments and rather nervously wiped the turf dust from her fingers with the corner of her apron.

'Will that be all, ma'am?'

Mother gestured with a hand and the girl left the room. As the door closed, Charles spoke:

'Well, goodbye.'

'Goodbye.' The word was thrown out with indifference. He moved towards her and bent to kiss her cheek, but she put up a hand and brushed his leaning face away.

'Spare me.'

He felt the heavy weight of hatred that he knew so well gathering in his stomach. Without a word he turned away from her and went over to the man on the sofa.

'Goodbye, father. You'll be fit again soon.'

An uncaring smile moved the old man's lips. Charles put a hand out and touched his father's shoulder in farewell.

'He would have become a man.'

'I am a man, mother, believe that.'

She threw her head back again and laughed. The sound of her laughter followed him out of the room, followed him for ever.

'I want to stay here,' said Diarmid.

'Impractical.'

'Right here.' He pressed his two hands down on the carpet, as if he were trying to make a hold for himself that no one could drag him out of. After a moment he looked nervously up at the old man.

'Have I annoyed you?'

'No. No, of course not. Bemused, rather.'

'Bemused,' repeated the boy, almost under his breath.

The gardener coughed and turned his back on them, stooping to grapple with some harmless daisies on the edge of the grass. The first rook launched itself from a branch and called mournfully down to its slower-witted companions. There was a general black stirring amongst the trees.

'It would merely lead to trouble.'

'I wouldn't mind.'

'I don't suppose you would. I have spent my life trying to avoid trouble. With a certain success, I must admit.'

The boy jumped up from the floor suddenly and threw his arms around the old man's neck.

'Look here, boy . . .' He looked down at the head pressed painfully against his ribs, felt the child's desperation impinging on his own private personality. Gently he put up his hands and tried to unknot the fingers laced at the back of his neck.

'Please.'

The old man groped behind him with a hand until he found the arm of a chair. He fell backwards into it and the boy came too, not loosing his grip for a minute. His face was now pressed against the drooping flesh of Mr Prendergast's neck.

'Please,' he murmured again.

'This is ridiculous. You're strangling me, boy. Consider. You're too old to be . . .'

The boy let go and crouched back on his heels, looking anxiously into the old man's face. 'Please.'

'Have some sense, child.' He rubbed the back of his neck which seemed to have taken the whole weight of the boy and was now aching. 'You can't come and live here. For one thing your parents wouldn't allow it.'

'They don't want me.'

The old man thought for a moment. 'I don't think it's quite that. They want you to be qualified to make your way in the world. Earn. Acquire knowhow. That's important, you know. I'm sure that they have your best interests at heart, no matter how things look to you.' He scarcely believed it himself as he said it. The thought of Sarah came into his mind. His heart, he recollected, had merely been filled with immense relief as he recognized the fact that here was a person that needed no propping or pushing from him, who preferred her own advice to that of others. Quickly he pushed the thoughts behind the nearest dusty curtain.

'You can't stay here,' he announced with authority.

'OK.'

To the old man's surprise the boy got to his feet. There was no arguing look on his face, merely blankness.

The other rooks had followed their leader now and the sky above the trees was filled with the rising and falling of black wings.

'It's time I went.'

'Yes.'

The old man groped around on the floor with one hand for the whiskey bottle. It wasn't within groping distance. He let the matter slide. He was tired. He couldn't think of anything to say. 'It was a wild thought. Panic. You didn't really mean it.' Wrong, weary words.

'I'll be seeing you,' said Diarmid coldly and left the room.

'Tttt.'

He was annoyed by the situation and with himself for having allowed such a situation to arise. Exasperated that even now, at the fag end of his life, after all his precautions, someone could touch him, make him feel uneasy pain.

Below in the garden Sean, panting each time he stooped, began to fill the barrow with weeds. Diarmid strolled around the corner as if he owned the place and crossed the path just by where Sean was working. He walked across the grass and, taking his penknife out of his pocket, began to cut a selection of roses from the nearest beds. For a moment Sean watched in silence, not believing his own eyes.

'Hey!'

The boy paid no attention. His knife cut obliquely through the green wood.

'By Jesus, I'll fix you.'

Sean picked up the rake, which leant against the half-full barrow. The old man pulled himself up out of his chair and went over to the window. He pushed it open and the sweet warm smell of summer evening gardens surrounded him.

'Sean. Leave him be.'

Sean didn't stop or look round. 'I warned him.'

'No matter, he's doing no harm. I told him he could bring a few flowers home to his mother.'

The gardener turned suddenly and walked back to the barrow. He threw the rake in on top of the weeds. 'You're the boss.' He picked up the handles of the barrow and wheeled it off down the path.

Diarmid watched him out of the side of his eye, then folded the knife up and put it into his pocket. With a sudden violent movement, he turned towards the house and hurled the roses at the window where the old man stood and then ran off down the avenue. The roses lay scattered on the lawn, red and yellow, flame and pink, colourful waste. Mr Prendergast waited until Diarmid was out of sight and then he went slowly out into the garden. With difficulty he picked up the fallen flowers and brought them into the house.

✳   ✳   ✳

He felt Clare's presence as soon as he entered the room. Any time that she had come into this room, she had balanced herself on the corner of the sofa like an awkward guest, rather than making herself at home in one of the armchairs. She was there now, her head bent towards a dark sock stretched over a mushroom. The silver splinter in her other hand glittered as it moved through the wool. She sighed as he passed her. She had never liked sewing. Without a word he sat down at the piano. His back was adamantly towards her but he could hear, from time to time, her sighs. A familiar exasperation prevented him from playing. He flexed his fingers in preparation but couldn't bring himself to place them on the keys.

'To what do I owe the pleasure,' he paused on the word,

rather like Diarmid might, tasting its insincerity, 'of this manifestation?' It was the sort of question he had plagued her with over the years. As she had grown older and less wounded by his grotesqueries towards her she had ceased to try and answer. There was silence in the room.

'A surfeit of alcohol might, I suppose, cause hallucinations.' He began, after a moment's consideration, to play with great precision a pavane. A rhythm, he decided, of suitable dignity for a moment like this. He played quietly.

A warning of approaching death? He shook his head in answer to his own question. The angel of death would be unlikely to arrive with socks to darn; of course, you never had much sense of occasion.

In the autumn of 1919 he had returned to Oxford to finish his studies, interrupted by the war. Clare's father had been a don with musical inclinations who had offered an open invitation to him to use the piano whenever he wished. Clare had always been around, little more than a child, but filled with a soft and tranquil admiration for him that was irresistible. The horror of the war he had survived hung about him like a thick cloak. He was incapable of throwing it off, seemed rather to rely on its denseness to protect him from the demands of living people. He had tired very quickly of university life, finding the self-confidence of the very young tedious and the desires of those whose lives, like his own, had been disturbed by war, to start climbing the ladder of success as soon as possible frightening. He was unable to find in himself any seed of either confidence or ambition. As he had left home that last time he had, in fact, been filled with anger that Alexander, the potential man of achievement, had not been the one to survive to face the hateful world. Taking Clare by the hand, he had begun to run. Now he realized that, in all their years together, he had given her nothing, only a child that he had not allowed her to enjoy. She had slowly died of starvation. In her whole life with him only her garden had been an act of defiance against his indifference. He was suddenly shaken by anger. Not against himself but against Clare that she had denied her own right to existence. He turned from the piano to speak to her once more but the sofa was empty.

'I am old,' he complained to the emptiness. 'I should not be tormented by the past like this.' He got up slowly and went to search for the whiskey bottle.

*　*　*

One day the good weather was gone. A wind from the west tossed the arms of the trees and forced Clare's rose bushes to dance ungainly dances. Shreds of pink, yellow and red chased each other over the wet grass.

Sean arrived at his usual time and shut himself in the potting shed without coming into the house for his cup of tea. When he did come into the kitchen at lunchtime, a smile lay on his face like a slice of moon in a turbulent sky. He was not given to smiling. It made the old man slightly uneasy. Sean sat down at his place in silence and smiled at his waiting meal. Mr Prendergast opened the paper.

'It's all over the town.' He always referred to the village as the town.

'What's that?' asked the old man, more out of politeness than interest. He moved the paper slightly to one side, so that he could see Sean's face.

'They're getting rid of the little brat at long last. It's

one decision they'll not regret, anyway.'

'I haven't the remotest idea what you're talking about.'

'That Toorish brat. He's off to Dublin first thing in the morning. If they had real sense it's to an institution he should be going.'

Mr Prendergast put the paper down on the floor by his chair. 'I've never found him any trouble.'

'Well, you're the only one for miles. Traipsing in and out as if he owned the place. Picking the mistress's roses. Giving out cheek.'

'I don't understand why you get so worked up about those roses. Flowers are for picking.'

'She and I made that garden what it is.'

'I'm not denying it.'

'And not for the likes of him.'

The old man looked silently at his plate for a moment. The paper on the floor sighed with boredom. 'Better that he should appreciate than no one. However, how do you know, anyway?'

'Amn't I after telling you. The whole town has it.'

'You never go near the village.'

'I do when it suits me.' He began to eat his lunch. He turned the fork upside down and packed the food on to it unusually energetically.

The old man couldn't bear to watch. 'It seems to me . . .'

Sean pointed the loaded fork across the table before shoving it into his mouth. He spoke with difficulty through the food. 'You only see what you want to see. Have a good look around the house before you say too much and see what he's laid his hands on. Cast your eyes round.' He chewed triumphantly.

'I think you're forgetting our relative positions. Taking liberties.'

'I certainly wouldn't want to do a thing like that.' He leant forward towards the old man. 'Everything'll be all right when he's gone. Just like it was before. You'll see. Just the two of us and a bit of peace.'

Mr Prendergast picked up his plate and took it over to the sink. He felt a cold lump forming in his stomach as if he had swallowed a large, cold stone. He recognized the feeling with alarm, like diagnosing an unpleasant illness. He remembered the same physical symptom from his childhood. It was hatred . . . He swept the untouched, dead pieces of food off his plate into the bucket with a fork. He couldn't bring himself to speak to Sean. So it had been with Alexander, the feeling you wanted to pull the stone out of your gut and crush someone with it.

Sean's chair scraped on the linoleum and his boots tapped across the room to the door.

'I didn't want to upset you,' he whined, knowing too late that he had pushed his luck rather far. 'Sir.' He coughed a little, waiting for some reassurance, grasped the handle and opened the door. 'I only thought I ought to warn you, like.' He went out, at last, into the fine rain that was now drifting rather than falling through the blue air.

Mr Prendergast left the dishes to soak in the sink with the tail-end of a bar of Sunlight soap to cut the grease. He went upstairs to the old nursery and had his sleep in the chair by the rain-pearled window. Swallows scraped and twittered under the eaves, coming to grips with their northern world. He slept for a long time and awoke stiff and melancholic. Slowly he tidied the soldiers away into their boxes and put the dust covers back over the furniture. The room was asleep once more. The child had, somehow, halted for a while the inevitable, dreary process of dying. Now, as the last grey cover went over the last chair, he could feel the process beginning again. He locked the door and went downstairs.

It was choir practice evening. He put the nursery key back on its hook. His legs and back ached from stooping. He couldn't think of anything more disagreeable than playing hymns for an hour and undoubtedly being worked over by the Rector.

* * *

'This evening we simply won't take no for an answer.' Her hands fluttered like butterflies around his shoulders, her cheek brushed his. He stopped playing and turned his head slightly towards her so that she might get the breath of whiskey from him and, perhaps, falter. But not Eileen. Her hands came to rest on his shoulders.

'Eileen . . .'

'Not a word. We have made up our minds. We'll carry you off in our car and James can run you home. We never eat till after choir practice. The girl leaves us something cold. You couldn't expect her to stay in. You and James can have a . . . nice big drink and a good chat.'

'If you insist.' He was too tired to argue.

She removed her hands from his shoulders and, for a moment, he thought she was going to clasp them but she decided against it. In earlier years she had been given to expansive gestures of this sort. Never appealing, he remembered.

'That's settled, then. I'm so glad.'

Her hands fluttered around him again but, before she had time to touch him, the first ladies chattered into the church.

They captured him when the singing was over and walked,

one on each side of him, as if they thought he might escape, take to his heels across the weed-splashed gravel and out of the gate. The Rector's cassock flapped in a ridiculous fashion round his legs and his shoes needed a good polish. Politely the old man refused to sit in the front seat but they insisted, almost pushed him through the car door. His own car looked forlorn by the vestry door as they drove away.

'You'll have to have a word with the Brown girl,' said Mrs Evers as the Rector paused nervously in the gateway, ducking his head quickly this way and that to make sure that nothing would take him unawares.

'There's nothing coming,' said the old man irritably. The Rector continued to duck.

'I like to make absolutely sure,' he muttered. 'It's a blind corner.'

'She hasn't been coming to choir practice as regularly as she might. Do go on, dear. We can't sit here all night.'

The car moved across the road in a series of little jumps.

'Perhaps you, too, James, should take to shanks's mare.'

'I'm sure there's a young man involved. I haven't asked, mind you, but I would suspect. But I do think if she's going to continue to sing in the choir she ought to come to practice.' She tapped her fingers impatiently on the back of the seat waiting for him to speak. 'Don't you?'

'Quite,' answered the Rector automatically. He rubbed at the windscreen fretfully with the back of his hand. 'Can't anyone ever wash this windscreen?'

'It's on the outside,' said the old man. 'Flies and the like. Summer flies and dust, bird droppings, too, sometimes. Sean gives mine a rub from time to time.'

'We haven't had a man for years.'

'It would come better from you than me.' The Rector appeared to hear his wife for the first time.

'What would?'

'A word to Joanna Brown. Before things go any further. The young slip from the church, if allowed. Have you got your bobby dodgers on?'

'No need.'

'That car had.'

'Tttt.'

'Someone mentioned to me, just in passing, that the young man wasn't altogether suitable. How is dear Sarah?'

'I presume she's all right. She doesn't correspond. We don't.'

'She used to write to Clare. I remember how pleased she used to be to get her letters.'

'It's a duty she doesn't feel bound to continue with me.'

The rectory was Victorian, an agglomeration of peaks and towers, turrets and tiny spires, Gothic windows and expansive bays, surrounded closely by giant rhododendrons and, in the summer, a mist of midges.

'It's too wet, alas, for you to come and give us some advice about my borders.'

'My dear Eileen, you know I've never been a gardener.'

'I thought that a little of Clare's knowledge might have rubbed off on you.'

The Rector stopped at the hall door and bowed his head over the steering wheel for a moment, as if he were saying grace.

'I'm afraid not.'

'The back of my neck is stiff,' complained the Rector.

'You will insist on sleeping with the window open.'

'Tttt.'

They got out of the car, each one with difficulties of his own, and went into the hall.

Eileen turned the light on. The light hanging in the centre of the hall was covered by a shade of multi-coloured glass, which made the walls and furniture multi-coloured also. The three old people took on the look of over-elaborate stained glass. They stood awkwardly for a few moments, not quite knowing what to do next. Then Eileen gave one of her charming laughs and almost clapped her hands again. 'It's so nice to have you here at last.' Her face was marbled green and red. 'Run along both of you into the sitting room and have a drink. I'll join you in a minute.'

She looked at her husband as she laid a delicate stress on the word 'drink' then, like a demon in a pantomime, she disappeared into a dark hole in the wall. The Rector gestured to the old man to follow him into the sitting room where a turf fire smoked wearily on the hearth.

'Take a pew.' The Rector laughed, then stopped abruptly and watched while Mr Prendergast lowered himself into an armchair that in the distant past had given more support to brittle bones. 'Sherry? Whiskey?'

'Whiskey.'

Only the Rector's unpolished shoes and the whisper of the fire broke the silence.

'It must be several years . . .' The Rector came across the room and handed him a glass. Pale amber, too pale amber.

'Not since Clare . . .'

'That's right. We miss Clare. How stupid of me to say that to you. You must know about that. She was such a . . . tower of strength.'

James Evers could no more pour a drink than preach a sermon, that was for sure. The old man got up. 'Do you mind?' He went over to the cupboard where the bottles were. He smiled back, disarmingly, at the Rector over his shoulder. 'A drink must be a drink.'

'Go ahead, old man. Help yourself.' He wandered round the room looking for nothing. 'A tower of strength,' he repeated.

The old man took a sip of his drink. An improvement. 'You surprise me. She always seemed remarkably diffident to me. Almost nervous. Too nervous.'

'No, no, I assure you. You've only to ask Eileen. A very font of wisdom.'

'Fount.'

'Fount,' said the Rector irritably.

The old man took another sip and looked out of the window. It was almost dark. The rain had stopped but the wind stirred the rhododendrons. The green leaves moved like a thousand wings. 'Why don't you cut those bushes back a bit? They're crushing the house.'

'There's no view from here, anyway. Not like over with you.'

'How can you breathe with them all pressing round you like that?'

'We don't notice it.'

'My mother planted them all over the place. An appalling Victorian vice. I always wanted to root them out but Clare liked them. Rhododendrons.' He spoke the word with contempt.

'Ireland wouldn't be Ireland without its rhododendrons.'

'What utter rubbish.'

'Tell me one thing, Charles.' The Rector poured himself a small glass of sherry. He splashed a few drops on to the front of his cassock and rubbed at it with disgust.

'Yes?'

'This withdrawal.'

'You wouldn't have so many flies, either. Midges. In the summer. I always remember the midges here in summer evenings. It's all that shrubby mess right up to the house.'

'There seems to be something – well . . . a little, don't take me amiss . . . unnatural about it. As an old friend, I feel I can speak to you like this.'

'All round the tennis courts, flies. Drive you insane. Walking through your hair in thousands. I don't suppose you keep the court up these days, though.'

'We feel, Eileen and I . . .'

The old man turned round from the window. 'I do not wish to discuss my way of living. Or dying.'

A nervous giggle burst from the Rector. 'Dying doesn't come into it, old man. You've many years ahead of you yet. Please God, as the . . . ha-ha . . . others say.'

The old man sighed. 'At some point in our lives we cease to grow and start to decay. It's an inescapable fact. I passed that point more years ago than I would like to say. I would like to die as I have tried to live, in private.'

'Alone?'

'If you prefer to put it that way, yes, alone.'

'All in the dark,' said Eileen, switching on the light as she came in. 'I'll have a tiny sherry, James. Do look at that fire. You've let it almost out.' She ran to the fire in case it died before she got there and threw herself down beside it. The bellows blew a golden hole in the centre of the turves.

'Ah, Eileen.' The Rector was relieved.

'I expect you're both starving. I'll drink my sherry quickly and we can go in.'

'We were just . . .'

'Quite,' said the old man. He jerked his head towards the whiskey. 'May I?'

'By all means.'

'We were just . . . ?' asked Eileen, sitting back on her heels and looking up at them. Her finger tips had become white with turf dust.

'Well . . . ah . . . yes . . . talking about Clare, actually.'

'Dear Clare.' She rubbed her fingers on her skirt.

'I was saying to Charles that she was a tower of strength.'

'Indeed she was.' She took a little swoop at her sherry and spilt some down the front of her dress. 'Oh, dear.'

'You're so clumsy, Eileen,' moaned the Rector.

'Arthritis.' She held her gnarled fingers out towards the old man. 'It's very hard for me to get a good grip on things sometimes. Occasionally I break things. James gets so angry.'

'I don't.'

'Yes, you do.' She wagged a finger at him. 'Frequently.'

'One has so little left.'

'We've given all the silver to George and Hilda. Not that I suppose they use it. People don't these days. I'll have to ask you for a hand up.'

The Rector gave a hand to his wife and she got slowly up. There was a crackling of bones, like dry sticks being consumed by fire.

' "Come away, come away, Death, and in sad cypress let me be laid." ' For no good reason, Alexander's voice was in his head. No interference, a clear line from Paradise. There were no cypress trees in the graveyard. Three chestnut trees shaded the leaning stones. In the spring the pink candles glowed as sweetly as the pyramids of candles the others lit in their churches in supplication and appeasement.

'Charles.'

The Rector's voice startled him. 'Oh . . . ah . . . yes?'

'Where were you?'

'I'm sorry. I drop off sometimes. Like a horse, I must be able to sleep on my feet.'

The Rector's wife put her arm through his and gently pulled him towards the door. 'We'll go and eat.'

They walked in silence through the multi-coloured hall to the dining room. Cold meat and beetroot sat gloomily on three plates, longing to be eaten. They all sat down and the Rector bowed his head and muttered a few Latin words. Mr Prendergast carefully placed his glass in the exact centre of a lace mat on the table, slightly to his right. The Rector took the lid off a dish; steam billowed up into his face.

'Ah. King Edwards. Our own. I guarantee they're delicious. Help yourself.' He handed Mr Prendergast a spoon and pushed the dish in his direction.

'Thank you.'

'Beetroot always reminds me of graveyards,' said Eileen, chopping nervously with her fork.

'I don't know why we have them so often.'

'They're easy to grow and difficult to sell. I sell a lot of the garden stuff down in the village, you know. Helps make ends meet. But really one finds they only want cabbage and carrots, perhaps some onions now and then, or cauliflowers. Terribly dull. They've so little imagination. Since I've had to give up golf

I like to have some excuse to spend time out in the air.'

'I didn't know you'd given up your golf.'

She waved her hands towards him without speaking.

'I'm sorry.'

Disarmed by this second of sympathy, she plunged. 'Have you never thought of going to live near Sarah?'

'I can't say I have.'

'A nice little flat in Kensington or somewhere. Central heating. That's what would appeal to me. Not the constant struggle in the winter here to keep the circulation moving. Sarah could pop in. It's not right you being all on your own the way you are.'

'I haven't the faintest intention of moving to Kensington.'

'You could probably get a fair price for the house if you went the right way about it.' She leant towards him confidentially. 'I'll tell you something. If James dies before me, and please goodness he won't, I shall go straight over to George and Hilda. I know they'd want it.'

'I am perfectly happy where I am. In my own home.'

'I don't want to interfere . . .'

'I've often wondered since that day how your lunch guest got so wet.' The Rector, tactfully, was changing the subject.

'Swimming.' The old man's voice was ice cold. He stood up. 'I will be going now. It was kind of you to invite me but I would appreciate it if, in future, you would . . .'

'Quite,' said the Rector.

Eileen was distressed. 'But Charles, you mustn't be angry. Believe me, we only have your interests at heart. And one tends to think of Clare, of what she would have wanted.'

'Clare would agree with me. I should be allowed to get to hell, or wherever, in my own way.'

'Charles. Sometimes you say such terrible things.'

'No need for outrage. I appreciate your . . . ah . . . thoughtfulness. If you'll excuse me now, I think I'll be getting along.'

Eileen was crying unashamedly into the beetroot.

The old man sighed with exasperation. 'It is the incompleteness of women that drives me mad,' he said to no one.

'I'll drive you home,' said the Rector.

'I prefer to walk, thank you.'

'Clare was so devoted to you. All those years, never a word against you, never a complaint, and you were never the easiest . . . You sound as if you hate her. It's so unfair. Ungrateful.'

'What should I be grateful for? She gave me nothing.'

'Devotion.'

'A dog can do that.'

The Rector's religious hand touched his sleeve. 'I'll drive you home.'

'She gave you a child.' Her voice was becoming shrill.

'We're too old for this kind of conversation. Now, if you'll excuse me . . .'

'It's raining,' said the Rector.

'I'll go along the back lane. It won't take more than ten minutes. A little rain never hurt anyone.' He looked at Eileen rubbing at her eyes with her napkin. 'I appreciate your interest. I merely . . . I can't explain . . . words . . .'

She nodded bravely at him over the starched damask.

'Goodnight.'

'Goodnight.'

'Goodnight, James.'

'Goodnight, old man.'

'Sunday, morning and evening.'

'Quite.'

The back lane passed the yard gates of both the rectory and Mr Prendergast's house. Along one side was an embankment, on top of which ran the railway line, now unused, the narrow gauge hidden by brambles and cow parsley. In his childhood, the old man recalled, if there were anyone on board for the house, the driver would stop the train just above the yard gate and a couple of the men would be waiting in the lane to help the visitors down the crude steps that had been cut in the bank. This saved a tedious drive to the nearest station and gave both the visitors and the Prendergast boys a feeling of enormous importance, as if the whole railway system was run especially for them.

'How good it is,' Alexander had said to him one afternoon as they watched the little balls of smoke jerking up into the sky before the engine got under way again, 'to be people of privilege.' They used to walk for miles, one on each shining track, arms outstretched to balance, stopping every ten minutes or so and kneeling down, ears to the rail, listening for the vibrations that meant a train was on the line. Then they would slide down into the long grass of the embankment and wait until it went past. Goods trains rolled slowly along the track leaving a smoky, dungy smell behind in the air and usually the sound of worried sheep or cattle. Sometimes it was possible to climb on to the last truck and sit there, rocking from side to side, feet dangling, watching the rails and sleepers unfolding behind you, until you became bored, or you were getting too far from home. Alexander, usually preoccupied with his own thoughts, might as well have been on his own really, except that, every so often, at some bend in the lane or some fence that had to be climbed, he would pause, tapping one foot impatiently on the ground and humming to himself until the younger boy had caught up with him.

The old man was drenched by the time he reached home. He climbed up the back steps and in through the kitchen door. He was concentrating so hard on removing wet shoes and stuffing them with paper, shaking and hanging up his coat, mopping at his face and neck with a towel, boiling a kettle for a hot whiskey and a hot water bottle, working hard, in fact, on the survival routine, that he never felt the imperceptible change in the atmosphere that tells you that there is someone other than yourself in your normally empty house.

✳   ✳   ✳

He slept later than usual and lay for a few minutes after waking, conscious only of the deep aching in his bones, across his shoulders, down his arms, even his ankle joints felt as if he would never be able to use them again. He thought about a flat in Kensington, warm towels on a rail in the bathroom, a lift with wrought-iron gates, only a short walk, leaning on a rubber-tipped stick, to the public library, deference from men wearing gloves and rows of ancient battle ribbons, outside clubs and theatres, men of the old school who knew a gentleman when they saw one. Sarah would visit him once a week and they would both be faced with the almost impossible creation of a relationship which neither of them were exactly eager for. He opened his eyes, preferring the reality of the wreck of his bedroom. Outside the sky was a pale wet blue, the branches of the trees stretched sideways with the wind. Another day to see through. More rain would come, more petals would blow on to the grass, more chords from the piano would stroke the air, another night would wipe the colour from the sky. I could end it now, he thought, if only I was not afraid of what I might find.

He got himself out of bed, partially dressed himself and shaved the white stubble from his chin. He had all his own teeth which he cleaned each day with care but his gums bled with the pressure of the brush and the globs of blood on the white basin made him feel ill. A door banged somewhere and he stood still, his razor in his hand, listening, mildly surprised. There was no further sound, so he continued to scrape his face, stretching the skin carefully between the fingers of his left hand. The manifestations around him recently had not been ghosts of the door-banging, chain-rattling kind, merely pointing fingers of the past. He hoped vaguely that they weren't going to change their tactics and become uncomfortable to live with.

He went downstairs and put the kettle on and lit the grill for toast. He opened the kitchen door. The air smelled of wet grass. Sean was weeding within calling distance. 'Morning, Sean.'

'Good morning. You're on the late side. You had me a bit uneasy.'

'Overslept. I've the kettle on, if you're feeling like tea.'

'I'll be with you in a minute.'

He paused on the top step, scraping the mud off his boots before he came in. 'It's not like you to sleep in.'

'I think maybe I'm getting a cold.'

Sean collected his mug and sat down. He stirred in three teaspoonfuls of sugar, clattering the spoon against the sides of the mug. 'At this time of year?'

'You can catch colds at any time of year.'

'I don't feel too good myself.'

'We're getting on.'

'Sometimes I feel there's not long left in it for me.' He gave a melancholy sigh, blew on his tea and proceeded to suck it into his mouth.

The old man spread some marmalade on a piece of toast. He couldn't bring himself to sit down with Sean so he moved nervously around the kitchen as he ate it.

'There's ructions below.'

'What is it this time?'

'What you might expect. Didn't the boy run away in the night. Neither sight nor sign of him to be seen anywhere.'

'My goodness,' said the old man uneasily. 'I wonder where he's got to.'

'You might well ask,' said Sean.

There was a long silence. Sean bided his time, staring at the leaves whirling round on the top of his tea. The old man thought about doors that bang in the morning and wondered what to say next. Silence, he decided, was the best line to take.

'I wouldn't say he'd be a hundred miles away.'

'He'd hardly have had time . . .'

'You know well what I mean.'

'I don't think so.'

'I'm not blind, you know.' He drank some more tea. 'Don't think I haven't seen what's been going on.' He stared the old man maliciously in the face. 'I've eyes in my head.'

'I really don't know what you're talking about.'

'No?'

'No? If you've finished your tea . . .'

'I haven't.'

Mr Prendergast turned his back on the gardener and buttered himself another piece of toast. It wasn't going to be a day like any other.

'I always used to wonder to myself why you and the mistress never got on.'

'I don't want to hear any more of this sort of talk. You may go now, whether you've finished your tea or not.'

Sean pushed the cup across the table with a tip of one finger; it left a trail of brown liquid behind it. 'You're not natural.'

'You're fired.'

'Ha-ha-ha.'

'I've taken enough of your insolence and laziness over the last few years. I'm not taking any more.'

'Laziness?'

'That's what I said.'

'Who made that garden what it is?'

'My late wife.'

'And my work. My hands. My humping earth on my shoulders from here to there. Never a night I didn't go to bed tired out in every bone.'

'It was your job.'

'I was hired as a chauffeur.'

'And a good job you made of that, if I may say so.'

The gardener screamed and clutched his head between his earthgrained hands. 'May God forgive you.'

'He has a lot to forgive us both for.'

'To throw that in my face.'

'I'm sorry,' said the old man, surprising himself with his gentleness. 'But you've been trying hard to make me angry. You may not realize what you've been insinuating . . .'

'Not a word but the truth has passed my lips. Insinuating, is it? The truth. I seen it for years and I never recognized it till now. And if it's sacking me you are, the guards will be only too pleased to hear the truth.'

'If you don't get out of here this instant . . .'

'What about my wages?'

'I'll send you a cheque.'

'And the pension she promised me when I retired?'

'You should have thought of that before you started on this madness.'

Sean picked his cup up from the table and threw it on to the floor. It broke in four pieces and thin streams of brown tea snaked across the linoleum. He got up and walked to the door without a word. He opened it and stood quite still, quite silent, looking out at his garden, at the wind-stirred rose bushes, her shrine, his appeasement, his only life. The old man ignored him. He bent down, with pain, and picked up the broken pieces of china. A question came into his mind. He dropped the pieces, one by one, into the bucket. His head throbbed with the stooping.

'Not natural, you said?'

'That's right.'

'What precisely am I to understand by that?'

'You can understand what you like. Others will have no trouble in knowing what I mean.'

The old man pushed a laugh out of his throat. It would have fooled no one. 'I take it you're accusing me of some sort of immoral behaviour.'

'Unnatural.'

'You must really be mad. You'd better go. Don't worry, I'll send you a cheque.'

'Taking into consideration . . .' He suddenly sounded unsure.

'Absolutely nothing. Get out. Now.'

'It's a mercy she's dead.' He closed the door behind him softly with an unexpected element of civility.

The old man watched him down the steps and along the path to the potting shed. His feeling of anger was completely swamped by a feeling of great relief at having finally got rid of Sean. The garden could go to hell for all he cared. It was merely a relic of the past. Once Sean was out of sight he turned to look at the hooks where the keys were hanging. The nursery key was not there. He turned on the tap and squeezed out the floor cloth under it and, stooping down, wiped the mess of tea and unabsorbed sugar from the floor. He rinsed the tea from the cloth and took a cup down from the shelf above his head.

'I've brought you a cup of tea.'

The boy had taken the soldiers out of their boxes and the floor was a battlefield once more. Over by the window two armchairs had been uncovered and pushed together to make a bed. The shelves where the boxes had been were piled with food, arranged as if in a shop. A pyramid of apples, some tomatoes in a small box, a couple of boxes of processed cheese, some tins of evaporated milk, a neat arrangement of tinned fruit, a tin opener hanging from a hook, three sliced loaves in cellophane wrappers and about a pound of unwrapped butter sitting tidily on a white plate. The boy looked up as the door opened. He had been moving a group of Scots Guards. He didn't speak. The look of confidence on his face was barely skin deep. His eyes moved restlessly, like oil beads on water.

'You've settled in very nicely. Perhaps I was wrong. Maybe you are officer material, after all.'

'I can stay?'

'There seems very little alternative.'

The boy got up and made a rush at the old man. He threw his arms around him. 'I knew you'd let me stay.'

'You've spilled the tea.' He pushed the cup into the boy's hand. 'Drink it before it gets cold.' He went over to inspect the commissariat. 'You would appear to be intending to stay for some time.'

'That's right. No one will think of looking here.'

'I wouldn't be too sure about that, if I were you.' He sighed and settled himself down in one of the chairs. 'Well, first of all you'd better tell me what happened. The truth, mind you, not some hysterical invention created to pull the wool over my eyes.'

'It was just like I said and you wouldn't believe me.'

'It wasn't that I didn't believe you, it was just that I didn't see what I could do about it.'

'When I got home yesterday afternoon, she had the master there and the whole thing just blew up. Boom.' He stared at nothing, remembering. The cup in his hands tilted so that the tea ran right up to the edge and quivered there.

'Mind your tea.'

'What?' The boy looked down at the cup and straightened it. He sat down on the floor again and put the cup on the ground in front of him.

'Boom,' said the old man.

'Yes. She screamed like a pig was being killed and he went on and on about me as if I was some kind of a criminal. My father locked the shop and joined the party. Reprehensible, the master said. I suppose you know what that means.'

'Yes.'

'It was easy enough to get the meaning, anyway, even if you never heard the word before. As if he cared whether I went to school or not, any of us for that matter, as long as he gets his money. I told him, too.'

'Unwise.'

'He came up behind me and did what he always does at school when he's in a bait. He gathers a little handful of hair, tight in his fingers, and pulls till it comes out. You can't stop from crying out.'

'Boy . . .'

'So in the end they decided I must go today. It wasn't even soon enough for them.'

'Your father . . .'

'Him. It's as much as his life is worth to speak out of turn. He's sometimes not too bad on his own. I've never understood why people get married.'

'I can't help you there.'

'You should know.'

'I can't remember.'

'That's old age for you.'

'Maybe I never knew.'

'Anyway, you said the thing to do was run away . . .'

'Oh, God . . .' groaned the old man.

' . . . So, I ran away.' He gestured at the food on the shelves. 'He'll have a right job to get his books square this month.'

This was no time for jokes. 'And what, might I ask, is your ultimate plan?'

'I hadn't really got one. I hadn't thought much, beyond getting away. It was as lucky you weren't here last night or you might have sent me home.'

'Indeed, I might.'

'I thought maybe we could go to England.'

The old man started laughing.

'What's so funny?'

'Everyone seems determined that I should go to England. I don't mind where you go, boy, but I'm staying here.'

'What's there here?'

'You forgot my age. Anyway, I don't find it so disagreeable here.'

'I thought you didn't like it.'

'It's where I've spent more years of my life than any other place in the world. Youth and old age . . . senility, some people seem to think. Well, Colonel Toorish, so this is it?'

Diarmid jumped to his feet and saluted. 'Yes, sir.'

'A state of siege.'

'Is that what it's called?'

The old man nodded. 'There's just one alarming thing, Colonel, which may interfere with your plans. There has been a spy in the camp.'

'You know what happens to spies.'

'Under the circumstances execution is a little impractical.'

'We must put him out of action.'

Mr Prendergast thought about this for a while. He had suddenly started to enjoy himself. 'That might be arranged. Like everyone, he has an Achilles heel.'

'What's that?'

'I'll tell you another time. I'm going out for a while. Possibly a couple of hours. Get some food and things like that. Whiskey. You never can tell how long a siege may go on for. Some have been known to last for years.'

'God, that'd be great, wouldn't it?'

'I'd rather it didn't myself.'

What am I doing? Why am I behaving in this irresponsible way? 'It'll only end in tears, Charless.' Nanny sat by the fireplace endlessly sewing, snipping the thread between her yellow teeth, crackling with starch as her arm moved up and down. Once, when he had asked her why she called him Charless, she pulled him against her apron and kissed his hair. 'Isn't it your name, child dear?'

'I'll lock you in and take the key.'

Suspicion pushed all other emotions off the boy's face. 'You're not going to renege on me, are you?'

'What did you come here for if you didn't trust me?'

'I do.'

'I shall lock you in and take the key with me. I'll lock all the outside doors, in fact. Just to be on the safe side.' He took the key from the inside of the door and put it on the outside. 'Do you want to . . . you know . . . before I lock the door?'

Diarmid blushed, most un-colonel like. He shook his head. 'I'll be off, then.'

'It seems like you don't trust me, either.'

'I want to make sure. You might just be tempted to go downstairs and you never know you might meet someone.'

'There's no one to meet.'

'You can't be too careful.'

'If I promised?'

The old man thought of Sean's mean face. 'This time I'd rather be certain.'

The boy shrugged. 'Just as you please,' he muttered ungraciously.

* * *

Downstairs, Mr Prendergast locked the kitchen door. There was no sign of Sean moving in the garden. He collected five bottles of whiskey from the cupboard. That should put him right out of commission for several days. Three remained. Better get another half dozen. Never do to run short of booze in the front line. He felt in his pocket to make sure his cheque book was there. The car keys. He suddenly remembered that the car was at the church. 'Damn.'

Walking stick. A box. Impossible to secrete five bottles of whiskey on one's person. Or basket, perhaps. Keys. He'd already checked. A sure sign of nerves, checking and rechecking. Basket and stick clenched in one hand he went out of the hall door. He carefully closed it behind him, making sure it was locked.

A hole was blown momentarily in the solid grey cloud that hid the sky and a shaft of light passed across the façade of the house, startling the mica into trembling life. A great flower of happiness was growing inside him and as he stood on the top step he began to sing in his old man's voice:

'Voi che sapete . . .'

He went, still singing, down the avenue and cut off through the bushes, along an overgrown path that led, eventually, through the graveyard to the church.

He put the bottles carefully on the front passenger seat and then went round and settled himself into his own seat. The car was slow to start. The night in the open had done it no good. For about five minutes it made offensive coughing noises. The old man stopped pulling at the starter for a couple of minutes and just sat staring at the wheel. He wondered how he would treat the arrival of his old friend the Rector. The melody of 'Voi che sapete' wound itself through his thoughts. When he tried the starter again, the car engine came to life at once.

He drove to Sean's cottage. Hovel was a better name for it. Four thick stone walls, splattered with discoloured whitewash, held up a thatch that no one had tended for many years. The door and one small window let a minimum of light into a room where a couple of hens pecked hopefully at the mud floor when they got tired of pecking in the stone yard between the door and the road. The hovel crouched for support against a slightly larger building, now derelict. The slate roof had caved in in places and long green shoots of grass and weeds grew up through the holes, looking for the sun.

Clare had wanted to move the gardener into some unused back part of the house but the old man had been adamant about that. Sean on the premises was out of the question. The argument had meandered on for several weeks, he remembered, but had gradually petered out, like all Clare's arguments. She had little stamina.

He crossed the yard and, taking the bottles out of the basket, left them standing in a row, like soldiers, just to the right of the door. The hens showed no interest in the operation. They knew there was nothing in it for them. It was a neat plan, he thought, as he got back into the car; reasonably expensive, but guaranteed to keep Sean out of circulation for several days. A breathing space.

He drove to Roundwood, about fifteen miles away, where he cashed a cheque in the bank, bought several days' supply of ham and some whiskey, filled the car with petrol, in case of emergencies, and bought a toothbrush for Diarmid who, he decided, had probably been too obsessed by food problems to think of toothbrushes. Probably never brushed his teeth, bloody peasant that he was. Eight faces out of ten in the whole country filled with rotting teeth. Finally, he went into the hotel and stood himself a large whiskey.

'Well, oh well, oh look who's here. If it isn't Charlie Prendergast. Thought you were — ha-ha-ha-ha-ha — dead years ago.' A small man with a moustache focused two watering eyes on him with the greatest difficulty. 'Could have sworn we sent a wreath or something.'

Mr Prendergast smiled coldly, an almost dead man's smile. 'Clare.'

'By God, you're right. How bloody awful of me. People go so quickly these days. Hard to keep track. What? Never see you out and about anywhere. Become a bit of a recluse, hey? Can't say I blame you.' He pushed his drink along the bar until it stood companionably beside the old man's. 'Still living in that great big place?'

Mr Prendergast nodded.

'My dear fellow, you have my sympathies. We sold up a couple of years ago. Couldn't keep the place going at all, what with one thing and another. Bloody place needed reroofing. Can you imagine? I mean to say.'

They both stared at their drinks for a moment, thinking of acres of lead, tiles, timber, guttering. The man with the watering eyes sighed and pulled at one side of his moustache.

'Sold it to a fellow from Dublin. Business type. Nouveau. Very nouveau. Vous comprenez.' He winked across his glass. 'Goes up and down every day. Must be mad. Actually, taken all in all, he's not a bad chap. Eldest daughter hunts. Pity to see the old places going. We built ourselves a bung. All mod cons. Just outside Annamoe. Marjory's happy there. How do you manage to keep it on, hey?'

'I only use a couple of rooms.'

'I expect your girl'll sell it when you're gone. Once they get out they never really want to come back.'

'I suppose so.'

'Knock that back, old boy, and have another.'

Mr Prendergast obliged. Why not, after all? You might as well start an adventure drunk as sober.

'Two more of the same there, Barney.'

'Right you be, sir.'

'I've a boy in the States, another out in Ghana. He was at the Bar but decided there was no future in it, so up sticks and off he goes to Africa. My God, I said to him, all the whites are pulling out of Africa now, my boy, not like it used to be. Bloody fine place it used to be, too. What do you want to go poking your nose in for –? I said.'

'But he went.'

'Sure enough. Told me to mind my own bloody business. Something like that. You know the young. Always know best. Mind you, to give him his due, he seems to be doing very well out there. Next thing you know he'll come back with a black wife. Hahahaha. Marjory's face. Oh, ah, this'll interest you now. My youngest girl's married to Connolly Fitzherbert's boy. Remember old Connolly?'

'Haven't given him a thought for years.'

'Still going strong. Better shape than you or I. Doesn't do too much of this.' He flicked at his glass with a fingernail. The barman looked over from the other end of the counter. 'A bit deaf, though. You used to see a lot of him, didn't you? Played golf together, hey?'

'That was my brother. Alexander.'

'God, yes. Of course it was. Alexander. Yes, Handicap about five, I remember. He went in the Dardanelles, didn't he?'

'Gallipoli.'

They drank in silence for a moment. Their heads filled with the soft booming of distant guns, names, voices, faces of the past.

'Ah, yes,' sighed the man with the watery eyes.

'Quite,' sighed Mr Prendergast.

'Things have changed a lot since then.'

'True enough.'

'You know, now I've never said this to a soul before, but I'd never have believed we'd have made a go of it the way we have.'

The old man looked at him, puzzled. 'We?'

'You know, the Irish. Dev and all that lot. I bet you never thought back in 1916 that things would turn out like this.'

'I never gave it much thought.'

'Neither did I, old man.'

They both started laughing.

'How about another?' asked the old man when they had recovered.

'Why not?'

'The same again, Barney.'

'The same it is.'

It was quite some time later. The man with the sore eyes must have been having difficulty in seeing, only threads of blue showed among the folds of skin. Mr Prendergast's hands were as steady as two rocks. He felt on top of the world.

'I feel on top of the world.'

'Capital. Nothing like meeting old friends. A quiet drink or two. Tell you what, old man, why don't you come back to the bung and we'll give Marjory a surprise? Hey? How about that?'

A thought nudged Mr Prendergast. He shook his head. 'Can't.'

'Why ever not? You said you spend all your time playing the piano. Highly ad . . . mirable. Come and play our piano for a change. Nothing I like better than a bit of Chopin. Hasn't been tuned for years. Marjory insisted on bringing it. Damn foolishness, I said, but you know women. Anyway, come along.'

'I have an appointment somewhere,' said the old man vaguely.

'Keep up your tennis court still?' asked the new old friend, surprisingly.

Mr Prendergast thought about the tennis court with difficulty. 'Good God, no.'

'Remember those tennis parties the old lady used to give? Remember them, hey?'

'I can't say I do. I never enjoyed them. I remember that much.'

'You never were much of a chap for sport.'

'I suppose not. Never been gregarious.'

'Not like Alexander.'

'No.'

'Ah, dear.' The thin blue lines disappeared for a moment. He rubbed a finger up and down his cheek. 'The flower of England's youth and Ireland's, too.'

'Just water under the bridge.'

'I suspect you're a cynic. Are you a cynic, hey?'

'I don't think so. I find it hard to be very enthusiastic about the human race.'

'A cynic. That's what I'd call you. Have another drink?'

The old man shook his head. 'I think not, thank you. I fear I have delayed too long as it is.'

'Just as you wish. I won't press you. I'll just stay and have one for the road. May as well be hanged for a sheep as a lamb, hey?'

'Give my regards to . . . Marjory.'

'Barney. She'll be delighted . . . surprised, really, I suppose. Drop in, old man, any time you're passing. Anyone'll tell you where the bung is. Give us a bit of Chopin. Ah, Barney. Sure you won't change your mind?'

'Positive.'

'One of the same ilk, then.'

'Right you be, sir.'

Mr Prendergast drove the car with great care just out beyond the edge of the town. He stopped by the side of the road and switched off the engine. He felt definitely the worse for wear. Strange it was, he thought, as his capacity for drink appeared to be limitless in the emptiness of his house that he should be so affected now. Couldn't even remember the fellow's name. Remembered his place, though. A grey building, remarkable for its numerous chimney stacks which pushed great fistfuls of chimneys up into the sky. In the winter, when the smoke twirled up from most of them, the place had taken on the look of some sort of power house, rather than a dwelling. In latter years Clare had visited them from time to time and had usually come home with precious cuttings which she and Sean had nursed with love and stimulants until they began to thrive. The thought of Sean sobered him. He must get home. The boy locked up. He would drive very slowly and with great care. He must get home. Tucked right in to the left-hand ditch and then neither he nor anyone else would come to any harm.

*　*　*

It was well after five by the time he reached home. The hours had slipped through his fingers like wet soap. There was no sign of Sean for which the old man was thankful. It was going to be a beautiful evening. The solidity of the clouds had broken, the wind had blown itself out, the earth sighed contentedly beneath his feet. Indoors it was cold, evening, grey and dirty. He bolted and chained the hall door behind him carefully. The three flights of stairs seemed like Mount Everest. An almost impossible feat, to be celebrated at the top groping in one of the boxes and opening one of the bottles. Down the passage Diarmid rattled the handle and banged with his feet on the door.

'Coming.'

His head was shaking violently and the whiskey trickled out of the corner of his mouth. He breathed deeply in and out, trying to collect himself. This ridiculous way of carrying on, he thought, will be the end of me. I am too old for adventures. He took another drink and was surprised to see, out of the corner of his eye, Alexander, dressed for tennis, crossing the landing below. His whites were, as usual, immaculate. He smoothed his yellow hair back from his forehead with his right hand—a gesture he had frequently used, a self-satisfied gesture. He ran down the stairs, the rubber soles of his shoes squeaking slightly against the edge of each step. The old man replaced the top on the bottle and, bending cautiously down so as not to upset his equilibrium, he put it back in the box.

'Coming.'

He called louder this time, exasperated by the continuing rattling on the door. He felt unable to lift the boxes, so he left them at the top of the stairs for Diarmid to collect.

'Where were you?'

'I said I'd be a couple of hours.'

'You've been all day. I thought you'd had an accident. I thought . . .'

To the old man's horror the boy's eyes overflowed and tears ran down his pale cheeks. He turned his head away. Mr Prendergast put his arm round the boy's shoulders.

'I am sorry. I became involved in an irrelevant episode.'

'You've been drinking. That's what you've been doing. I can smell it off you.' His voice had become shrill and hysterical, like his own imitation of his mother. He pulled himself away from the old man and wiped at his face with his shirt sleeve. 'Anyroad, I'm bursting.' He ran out of the room.

'Take care,' called the old man after him, seeing in his mind's eye the strange meeting that might take place between Alexander and Diarmid.

'What of?' called back the boy.

'Nothing. Don't mind me.'

* * *

It was impossible to get away from the smoke. Even if the wind got up, it merely seemed to blow more smoke in your direction, never blow your personal smoke away. The sun, red through the smoke, was sliding down behind a few torn trees. The men's eyes stung, their throats itched, their bodies stank. The only thing that didn't taste of smoke was what you swallowed from the furtively uncorked flask. In the not very far distance a village smouldered. From time to time a dry beam would catch and send a spray of sparks up into the overcrowded sky. A field ambulance bumped along a narrow lane. In a ditch lay the bodies of six horses, waiting with eternal patience for a man with a spade and time enough to dig a large enough hole. The earth quivered as shells landed. Men moved through the smoke about their business, too tired to think that they might be taking their last step. Some of them played cards, some slept, some read crumpled letters, some sat and stared at the sky, now almost dark, but glowing with the reflection of a burning world. Some were just dead. When it was dark they would attack; out of the comparative safety of the trenches, across the fields and through what remained of the wood. The objective was the smouldering village, a push of about half a mile. For several days the tension had been mounting. Reinforcements had been filtering in. Diversionary tactics planned. The enemy at every moment had been under observation.

'Damn,' said a voice in the darkness.

'What's up?'

'I can't see a thing. We'll have to postpone the attack till the morning. First light.'

'Oh, sir . . .'

'I can't even see where my advance group have got to. I could have sworn I stationed them here by this chair.'

'Church.'

'Quite. Church, I meant.'

'We could turn on the light.'

'No. Better not. It could be seen down on the road. We don't want anyone snooping around. Things have gone so well. Send a dispatch rider off to HQ, will you, and let them know the form.'

'Right you be, sir.'

The dispatch rider set off along the lane, after the field ambulance, past the horses.

'I'm hungry, anyway,' said Diarmid.

'It's late.'

A cloud moved away from in front of the moon and white light lay in squares on the battlefield.

'You see. It would have been a massacre. No one can hide in that light. They have really got us where they wanted us. From the heights there.' He got up with difficulty from the floor.

'A massacre.'

'Death to many.'

'I know what it means.'

'I've seen it happen.'

'When you got your medal, was there a massacre?'

'I suppose you might call it that. I do wish you didn't want to be a soldier.'

'You were.'

'I had to be. I've never stopped regretting it.'

'I won't be massacred. I'll be the one who does the killing.'

'Precisely.'

'Wonder what it feels like to kill someone. Sometimes I dream about it. Someone you really hate.'

'Soldiers seldom hate the people they kill.'

'I bet I'll win more medals than you.'

'This is an abominable conversation. I thought you were hungry.'

'So I am.'

'Help yourself, then.' He waved a hand towards the shelves. 'I'll go down and make some coffee.'

'I'll come with you. I'd like to do that.'

'You know I'd rather you didn't.'

'Please. This once. I'll keep away from the windows. Please.'

The old man sighed. 'If you insist. I don't like it, though. Come on then, boy.'

He was glad of the boy's help climbing the stairs again. The firm hand under the elbow taking a little of the weight that now and then almost became too much for him. They brought up a jug of Nescafé which they laced with whiskey. It washed down the bread and ham adequately and made them both feel sleepy.

'Are you going to lock me in again?' asked Diarmid as the old man began to collect his things.

'I think it's best.'

'I don't like it.'

'I'm not trying to make a prisoner of you. You do understand that, don't you? It's really to keep other people out. Someone just might come prowling around. You ought to trust me. I am only trying to do what I think is best.'

'I don't like it. You wouldn't like being locked in, either.'

'I suppose I would take the circumstances into consideration. Tomorrow we'll think up some better scheme. It's just that I like to feel in control, boy. You know, this way nothing can take me by surprise. Tomorrow we'll . . . I am tired now. This room is becoming oppressive.'

'I only came because you were my friend,' whispered the boy.

'Thank you. Get some sleep now. Remember we have to take that village in the morning.'

Diarmid smiled. 'Yes, sir.'

They saluted each other and the old man closed and locked the door. He carried the key downstairs and put it on his dressing table beside a dusty pile of pennies and halfpennies. His bed was unmade. He always tried to remember to make it in the morning. He hated the wrinkled greyness of the sheets, the

uncouth pillows. He sat down on it, nonetheless, and bent to unlace his shoes. Normally he put them carefully on shoe trees each night but now he couldn't be bothered. He let each shoe drop to the floor as it came off his foot and he lay back against the pillows. This had been Alexander's room. When he had come in here to sleep, at the beginning of Clare's illness, he had found a blazer, a tail coat and an army greatcoat hanging in the wardrobe. There had been nothing in any of the pockets, save the white grit of ancient moth-balls. He was surprised that they had been overlooked by mother. She had been so thorough with regards to everything else. Trunks had been neatly packed and sent off to some charitable organisation in Dublin. Not even a pair of socks, neatly rolled, had remained in any of the drawers or a handkerchief with an ornate 'A' embroidered in one corner. His papers had been burnt. His golf clubs, tennis racket, cricket bat, all had left the house for some unknown destination. So much debris. Unattached property. The bed became a boat, rocking him towards uneasy sleep. Mother had always eaten paper-thin brown bread and butter every afternoon at four and taken China tea from a massive silver pot, strained through a strainer into an opaque cup. After Alexander's death she had eaten it on the move, pacing round the drawing room, from one window to another, staring angrily at the unsympathetic sky, at the hateful, constant rebirth of nature. From the piano to the fireplace, her glittering fingers clamped round a fragile piece of bread, she strode every afternoon for over forty years, her mind absorbed by the past, by one man's brief and beautiful life. Her skirts, which had only been mildly shortened during the passing years, flicked against the legs of occasional tables and the fluted columns supporting potted plants or cascades of sweet-smelling garden flowers, according to the season, and her words flicked like whiplashes against the ears of any guests foolhardy enough to call between the hours of four and five. Father, who never went into the drawing room unless there were evening guests, would refer to 'your mother's post-meridian perambulation', but he never laughed when he said it or even smiled. His eyes would droop sadly at the corners and he would fidget nervously with his moustache and then, having let you know that he realized all too well what went on around the house, he would lower his head like a man entering a tunnel and dash on about his business. Debris, rocked from the back of his mind by the waves between wake and sleep. It had been his father's decline into illness that had driven him irrevocably away. The terrible vision that entered his head of having to live with someone who felt love and hate as strongly as she did. His father had protected himself by withdrawal behind a barrier of gentle dignity and silence. He had the strength that his son lacked. Useless debris. Clare's waiting eyes. The flashing of rings on pale hands. If only there was some way of disposing of the debris, leaving the mind neat and ordered, but more and more now the mess, the past, kept breaking through the barriers.

'Wer reitet so spät durch Nacht und Wind?'

His fingers struggled with the notes. It will be, it must be, even acceptable this time. There was no complaint. Exhausted, he fell asleep.

* * *

He was awakened by banging. It's the boy, he thought, struggling to open his eyes. Every morning they were held closed by thin ribbons of glue-like substance. When they were finally open he

realized that it was well day and that he was lying on his crumpled
bed fully dressed save for his shoes. His head was splitting and
someone was banging. Not the boy. Not possibly the boy. It
was the door knocker making the house tremble, making his
head throb. Could he answer the door in his socks? It was
something he'd never done before but he'd have to do it now if
he was to do it at all. He wondered about ignoring the whole
thing. True, whoever was there would go away all right but anyone
prepared to make that appalling noise would surely come back.
It was merely putting off the evil hour. He sat up and survived.
He reached out for the whiskey bottle on the table by the bed.
Kill or cure. It was an instantaneous, though, he realized,
temporary cure. He tucked his unpleasant shirt securely into his
trousers and made his unsteady way out of the room and across
the landing. There was no sound from upstairs. May it stay like
that, he prayed, and he could do without interference from
Alexander also. To meet him, immaculately dressed for civilized
life, on the stairs at this moment would be the last straw. For a
moment the knocking stopped and he could hear the crackling
of his own prehistoric bones; then, whoever was at the door
began to batter once more. As he started the unlocking process
the knocking stopped and the knocker breathed heavily, shuffled
his feet and cleared his nervous throat. It gave a certain amount
of courage to the old man, who opened the door with a small
flourish. The Rector stood outside.

'Well, hello,' said the old man. 'What's all the . . . ?'

The Rector visibly disapproved of the sight that met his
eye. He cleared his throat again, then swept his hands out
wide, away from his body, and let them fall to rest, exhausted,
against his black clerical mackintosh. 'May I come in?' He was

obviously suffering under a great strain.

'By all means.' He opened the door wide enough for James Evers to squeeze his way through. 'What can I do for you? We seem to be seeing rather a lot of each other these days.'

'It's complex. If we might sit down.'

They crossed the hall and went into the study. Mr Prendergast opened one of the windows. A mean little wind hurried in and set things rustling and rattling. He put a hand to his head to steady it.

'I apologize for the deshabille. I ... ah ... was asleep.'

'Quite.'

The Rector placed himself carefully in one corner of the sofa; his eyes scurried here and there furtively, looking for evidence. He took a deep breath. 'You'll have heard the rumours.'

'Rumours?' To be calm was the important thing.

'The Toorish boy has disappeared.'

'Sean did mention something to that effect. I never pay too much attention to what he has to say, though. Sometimes he's not quite at himself. It all goes back to the accident, you know. It plays on him on occasions.'

'The child has run away from home.'

'Oh, dear. I'm sorry to hear that.'

'His parents are, needless to say, distraught.'

'Of course, but I hardly see ...'

'Father Mulcahy came to see me ...'

'Oecumenism.' No time for jokes, bad jokes in particular. A terrible sign of nervous tension.

'As usual, you are going to mishandle this.'

The old man turned quickly but Alexander was certainly not visible behind him.

III

'I hardly think this is a joking matter,' said the Rector, sour as a lemon.

'I agree.'

They eyed each other silently.

'In what way can I help you?'

'There are other rumours that you have not heard.'

'I haven't seen Sean for several days.'

'Sean says that you sacked him.'

'That's true but irrelevant. He's been a thorn in my side for years.'

The Rector didn't speak. He seemed to be gazing past the old man out of the window at the waving branches and the soft hills, but he saw nothing.

'James,' said the old man gently, 'you came here to ask me something.'

'Rumour has it that the boy might be here. Informed rumour.'

'What on earth would he be doing here?'

'Sean has been spreading malicious and . . . ah . . . I must say . . . scandalous stories far and wide.'

'Sean, indeed.'

'So Father Mulcahy, a decent fellow, really, felt compelled to come and see me. He . . . ah . . . came around last night. Of course, I assured him that what he'd heard couldn't possibly be true. Yes.'

'I suppose I should thank you. Though I'm not absolutely certain . . .'

'We were both agreed that I should, at least, come and tell you what people are saying.'

There was a long silence.

'I always told you you were a fool,' whispered Alexander.

'Am I to take it that people are accusing me of being a . . .'

'Quite,' said the Rector hurriedly.

'I can assure you . . .'

'No need. Absolutely no need, my dear fellow.'

'I won't deny that the child came up here from time to time. He swam in the lake, browsed a bit among the books, listened while I played the piano. He was never any trouble. On the contrary, in fact.'

'He should have been at school.'

The old man waved his hands helplessly in the air. 'Boys.'

'Quite.' His fingers roamed for a moment on the surface of the sofa. 'I fear you have been . . . ah . . . perhaps, careless.' The hand moved to his head and the fingers wandered among the remaining silver wisps.

'I admit, certainly, to a certain, well, negligence. I suppose that's what one must call it. I just let things be. I made no serious enquiries about things.'

'With no thought for the consequences?'

'Consequences never entered my head. The boy was happy here. He appeared to appreciate some of my finer points. I could only let him be.'

'Is he here at the moment?'

'Have you any idea why he left home?'

'Ah,' said the Rector irritably, 'the usual sort of thing, I suppose. I think they didn't see eye to eye with him about his future. A brat, I suppose, who thought he knew everything. Father Mulcahy wasn't very explicit. It was just this disturbing element . . .'

'Which is ridiculous.'

'I agree. I said so. Unequivocally.'

They looked at each other, each seeing for the first time the pain written on the other's face. In the garden the birds filled the air with painless song. The Rector hauled himself to his feet.

'He's not here, you say?'

The old man gestured wearily towards the door. 'You are at liberty . . .'

The holy hands waved a negative. 'I'll be on my way. It's all been most unpleasant. Forgive me for . . .' he searched for the right word, '. . . intruding.'

They walked in silence across the hall. Mr Prendergast opened the door and the Rector stepped out into the bird-song.

'It's going to rain.'

'Probably.'

'That's a west wind. Always brings rain. Well.'

'Well?'

'I knew it would be all right. I said to Father Mulcahy that it was all a wild goose chase. The boy'll turn up soon enough. Bad pennies always do. By the way, I haven't said a word to Eileen.'

'Might upset her.'

'Quite. Well.'

He held out his hand. The old man shook it briefly.

'Goodbye, old man.'

'Goodbye.'

The old man shut the door and stood in the hall until he heard the car drive off.

* * *

Upstairs, all was not well. The boy sulked on his improvised bed.

'It's all hours,' he complained as the old man entered the room.

'Querulousness will get you nowhere. Have you never learnt to sleep with the window open, boy? The atmosphere in here is appalling.'

Without speaking, the boy got up and opened the window.

'I heard a car.'

'Alas, yes.'

'What's happened?'

'It was someone looking for you. The hunt is up.'

The boy's face changed. A look of excitement and delight chased the sullenness. 'Is that a fact?'

The old man nodded.

'Who was it? What did he say? It wasn't Mam, was it? What did you do?'

'Take your time, boy.'

Diarmid came across the room, skipping over soldiers, the barricades, the gun emplacements, the field ambulance and took hold of the old man's arm.

'Was it the guards?'

'Heaven forbid. It was Mr Evers.'

The boy looked puzzled. 'The Protestant minister? What's it to do with him?'

'I happen to be one of his flock. Father Mulcahy thought it more tactful for him to come. Bearding the lion in its den, you might call it.'

'And you hopped him out of it, quick?'

'Well, I wouldn't say that exactly. I think he left reasonably satisfied.'

'Isn't that great. They'll never find me at all.'

'I wouldn't be too sure. They're none of them fools, you know. Have you eaten?'

'Not yet. I was waiting for you. I get the creeps up here all by myself sometimes.'

'You'll never make a good soldier if you get the creeps too easily.'

'It's only being locked in like that. I hate it.'

'Well, you can come down later and help me carry up a mattress. I'll sleep up here tonight.'

'You're a great old stick.'

'Thanks. What do you want to eat?'

The old man mainly watched while the boy had ham and baked beans and thick slabs of bread and soft butter. He then opened a tin of pineapple chunks which he mixed with condensed milk and washed down the lot with a can of Coca-Cola. The old man had a quick strengthening nip of what was in his pocket. Diarmid lay back in his chair at last and held on to his stomach.

'God, that was great. The best meal I ever had.'

'I've known better, I must admit.'

'In the trenches?'

'I must admit that meals in the trenches were not of a very high standard.'

'What would you have, like?'

'Diarmid, sometimes you push me too far. I simply can't remember every appalling thing that happened in my whole life. It was . . . It was fifty-five years ago, or thereabouts.'

'Ah, go on, try. I'm sure you could remember if you tried. I'd like to know.'

The old man closed his eyes and tried, obediently, to think about meals in the trenches.

'If one had to be left,' his mother's voice was clear and cold, like the frost the night she died. 'I can't understand why . . .' Her basic manners prevented her from speaking the remaining words. At that moment, he remembered, her fingers cracked as she twisted her rings viciously.

'There is very little justice.'

'What?' asked Diarmid.

'Corned beef,' invented the old man. 'Quite a lot of corned beef. Roly-poly pudding and fruit cake sent by ladies in Hampshire to fill the cracks.'

'I'd like that.'

'Under other circumstances, perhaps.'

'We were going to attack at dawn, sir.'

'So we were. Someone had blundered, eh?'

'It looks like it, sir. Will I give the order for the attack to begin?'

'A small reconnaissance party, I think, first. I don't like it when the enemy is too quiet. A few reliable men.'

'Sir.'

He saluted and picked up his field telephone.

The war game continued until the evening, attack and withdrawal, smoke and confusion and pain. No one had time to bury the horses. Then they went downstairs and dragged a mattress up to the nursery and some pillows and blankets. The prospect of a night on the floor didn't please him but there seemed to be no alternative. While they ate their supper, the old man started in on the story of the Golden Fleece and the boy listened until his eyes would stay open no longer.

'That'll do for now.'

'Oh, no. Please go on.'

'You're asleep. I'll tell you more tomorrow. We'll find a book downstairs, fill in the gaps. A lot of it escapes me now. You go to sleep though, now, boy.'

After a while, when Diarmid had dozed off, the old man opened the door quietly and went downstairs. The piano needed tuning. He must send for a man from Dublin. This escapade must be brought to a reasonable end. Tomorrow. The priest, a man he had always recognized to be a man of integrity, was probably the person to approach. In all conscience I cannot throw the boy to the wolves. I will have to fight. That's tomorrow. He played the opening bars of the Erl King. His fingers had stiffened over the last couple of days and were grimed with dust from the floor.

'Wer reitet so spät durch Nacht und Wind? Es ist der Vater mit seinem Kind . . .'

He half whispered, half sang. His fingers laboured.

'No, boy. No. No. No.'

He played on.

'Er hat den Knaben wohl in dem Arm, er fasst ihn sicher, er halt ihn warm.'

'Oh, for God's sake, Chas, stop murdering Schubert and come and have a game of tennis.'

The old man shook his head. You can't play tennis in the dark. You do not exist. Let my hands fumble in peace. He continued to sing. A shadow fell across the page as he leaned forward so that his eyes could make out the crowding notes, a hand placed another book on top of the Schubert.

'If you insist on strumming, let's have something you can

play. Something charming and sentimental.'

His hands paused. Alexander moved from between the page and the light. How I hated you, thought the old man. How strange that, in all these years, this is the one emotion that I remember. What sickness of spirit have I suffered from?

'Play, boy. Get on, can't you?'

His hands began to play once more and, behind him, Alexander, in his prime, began to sing.

> Birds in the high hall garden
> When twilight was falling,
> Maud, Maud, Maud, Maud,
> They were crying and calling.

Two days later he had left for the front.

'Bravo.'

Mother always came when she heard him sing, or so it seemed. She had stood motionless in the doorway until the song was over. He heard the rustling of her dress as she crossed the room and kissed Alexander.

'You are in good voice today, my darling.'

A lover's, caressing voice.

The old man picked the book from the ledge in front of him and threw it across the room.

'What are you doing?'

Diarmid came into the room. His face was pale and half alarmed. 'I woke and missed you. I heard the piano. Are you all right?'

The old man was sweating and a pulse throbbed over his right eye, sounding like a drum inside his head. He stared at the boy.

'Can I get you something? Coffee? A drink? An Aspro?' The latter being his mother's prop in times of crisis.

'No, no. I'll be all right.'

'You look terrible. You're not going to die on me, are you?'

'Not just this moment.' He spoke almost regretfully. He held his hand out towards the boy. Diarmid came over to him and laid his own hand in the palm of the old man's.

'Look, boy, I may as well say it now, we've got to look at things straight. Both of us.'

'You're not sending me back, are you? I won't go. I can tell you that much.'

'Sssh.' He pressed the boy's hand to stop him from speaking. 'Just listen a while. Tomorrow morning I shall bring you down to Father Mulcahy. Preferably to your parents, I think. A man with whom we could discuss . . .'

The boy's face was in shadow and it was impossible to see what his thoughts were, but his hand in the old man's was like a stone.

'You must understand me. I will bring you. We will talk. We will all come to some agreement. I should have worked all this out before. A reasonable agreement. It should be possible to arrange for you to go away to school somewhere for another couple of years. A decent school. You'll find lots of things you want to learn in a decent school. I am prepared to give financial assistance. Between us all we must be able to find some acceptable solution.' He put a hand momentarily on Diarmid's head. 'You know as well as I do that staying here won't get us anywhere.'

'I like it here. I want to stay.'

'I think the time has come for us to be sensible about the whole thing. You mustn't be afraid. You'll never make a good soldier if you're afraid of a confrontation like this. We'll drive down in the Ford. You'll see. Everything will be all right.' The words were not convincing the boy. He was very tired. He could only repeat them time and time again. 'Everything will be all right. We'll drive down in . . .'

The boy pulled his hand away and went over to the window. 'You silly old man. I thought you were my friend.'

'I shouldn't stand in the window, if I were you. Someone might see you.'

'It doesn't matter any more, does it?'

'In a way, yes, it does.'

Diarmid moved from the window to the display table. He looked down at the medals.

'Well, what about it? Will you do as I say?'

'There's nothing else I can do, is there? There's nowhere for me to go. I thought you'd help me. Take me to England or somewhere, anyway, that no one could find us.'

'Tír na n'Óg. Mind you, they tend to send you back after seven times seven years, which has led to problems in the past. No jokes. This is neither the . . . it's not possible, boy. I'm only sorry that I've been so slow about the whole thing.'

'Can I have your medal?' He had opened the case and taken out the Military Cross.

'You can have them all, if you like. They're no use to me.'

Diarmid put the medal in his pocket. 'I only want this one.'

'You'll probably get one of your own some day.'

'Grocers' assistants don't get medals.'

'I've told you. Everything will be all right.'

'You don't know them. Everything'll be the way they want. I know.'

'Look,' said the old man, exasperated, 'I promise you, everything . . .'

'. . . will be all right.'

'You're a cheeky little brat.'

'And you're a silly old man.' His still childlike voice was shaking with a determined effort to keep from crying.

There was a very long silence. The furniture, the books, the dead roses on the mantelpiece, all waited. A fly, awakened by the light, buzzed angrily for a moment and then slept again. The old man wondered where the whiskey bottle might be. He groped behind him with one hand, trying to find the piano so that he might lever himself up. He caught a knuckle on a corner and gave a little gasp of pain. He tried again and this time grasped the edge and pushed without success.

Diarmid turned and came over to his side. His eyes were red-rimmed but there were no tears. He put a hand under the old man's elbow and helped him gently to his feet.

'Thank you.'

'You wouldn't give me the money and let me go to England on my own?'

'No, boy. I'm sorry.'

'I didn't think you would. I doubt if I'd have been brave enough to go on my own, anyway. Otherwise, I suppose I'd have gone right away in the first place.'

'I suppose so.'

'You'll take me back?'

'Yes.'

'You won't . . . ?'

'No, boy. I won't throw you to the wolves if that's what you're worried about.'

'OK. So.'

The old man was relieved. 'That's the boy.' He touched Diarmid's arm.

'I don't feel happy, though.'

'No more do I. But I do believe it's the only thing to do.'

They stood beside each other, just touching, without speaking, for quite a long time.

'Come,' said the old man at last, 'we'll have a drink on it. Life is filled, boy, with uneasy silences. The one thing you'll grow to realize, if you've any sense, is that silence, even uneasy, is better than speech. All this communication stuff they go on with nowadays is rubbish. Dangerous, misleading, rubbish.'

'I haven't a clue what you're talking about. Not that that's anything new.'

'One day you'll know.'

'Everything?'

'Alas, no.'

'Even after reading all these books.'

'Possibly they only confuse you. I've always found it impossible to leave them alone, though. My mind is like blotting paper. Sucking up other men's ideas but producing few of my own.'

'Then you must know a lot.'

'I forget a lot. I've forgotten what my wife looked like, among other things.'

'You're codding.'

'I'm not given to cod. The occasional passing joke. Not cod.'

The boy let his eyes move slowly across the morass of old grey face. 'I never know whether you're a little touched or not.'

'No matter. Let's go and celebrate the beginning of a new life.' The boy grimaced. 'I'll do my last bit of fighting for you. No medals this time, though.'

Arm in arm they left the room.

Sean moved across the terrace until he stood by the window, peering into the empty room. 'I have you.' His voice was blurred with drink and triumph. 'I have you on your hands and knees. Dirty old sod. Mam.' He looked up to where the mistress watched him, from beyond the stars and moon. 'Forgive me for the dirty word but I'll fix him for you.'

He shuffled back over the terrace and down the steps. He moved for a while through her rose beds. She had a little rubber mat, God love her, on which she used to kneel to weed. He had never been great on weeding but she never expected it of him and would kneel, like a woman in the chapel, completely absorbed, only her fingers moving. His eyes were burning in his head. He pulled his cap down over them to protect them from the damp night air. In the far distance a car changed gear, otherwise there were no night sounds. He set off for the village, his boots leaving dark tracks on the dew-pale grass.

'It's as if I'd never known her.'

It was a good couple of hours later and the two of them leant sleepily against each other on the old man's mattress.

'You've said that before.'

'Alcohol makes one repeat oneself. Forgive me.'

'Yer.' The boy yawned. 'I wish I'd never known my mother.'

'It's not my mother I'm talking about. It's my late wife, Clare.'

'I know. I only said I wish I'd never known my mother. I'm sure your Clare would have been pre ... fer ... a ... bell.'

'I never wanted to be a parent.'

'I hear them fighting through closed doors. She always wins. I even heard him cry once. You ever cry?'

'I don't remember.'

'He's harmless. Fecks the odd couple of dollars from the till. Where's the harm in that? Isn't it his money, anyway? He looks so scared when he's doing it, I always feel like hitting him. For God's sake, if you're going to do it, do it and enjoy it.'

'Never had to worry about money. I mean, not really worry. Not enough for, well, you know, flamboyance . . .' (the boy nodded, recognizing the word) 'but enough to get by on. See me out.'

'I cry.'

'You're a child still.'

'It's not so much the things they do to me. It's the things I see. Do you follow?'

'Keep your eyes shut.'

There was a silence while they both emptied their glasses and the old man refilled them. Then the boy laughed.

'I see you as a mad old man and the funny thing is, I like you. Why is that?'

'I suppose because you must be a mad young man.'

'I don't fall for your advice.'

'Advice? I never advised anyone, boy.'

'You've just told me to keep my eyes shut.'

'It's the only way to live, without too much pain, I mean. Believe you me, the great thing is to protect yourself. Keep yourself out of the way of the slings and arrows of outrageous fortune.'

'Have a heart.' The boy's face was flushed and his eyes swollen with tiredness.

'Shakespeare. To be or not to be, that is the question. Whether it is nobler in the mind to suffer the slings . . .'

'. . . and arrows.'

'Quite . . . of outrageous fortune. The greatest man.'

'I just don't know what you're on about.'

'Believe me, boy, neither do I. I used to be reasonably collected. But I think of late,' he rubbed at his forehead with a certain degree of petulance, 'senility is setting in.'

'Senility?'

'Mental decay owing to advancing years. It happens to the best of us.'

'I'm almost asleep.'

'And I.'

'I thought I'd never sleep, thinking about tomorrow. But . . .'

'The magic power of alcohol.'

'You never said a truer word.'

In the long silence they drifted towards sleep. Young and old breathed at different speeds, on different levels. The black windows stared at them. Someone moved and a glass was overturned. The comforting smell of whiskey filled the room.

❊   ❊   ❊

The bell on the Catholic church struck four and hurrying after it, trying desperately not to be left behind, the slightly deeper bell on the Protestant church. It had always been the same. No matter what adjustments the verger made to the clock he had never succeeded in encouraging it enough so that one day it might beat its rival by a neck and amaze the village.

Five minutes later Mrs Toorish opened the nursery door and looked into the room. Behind her Mr Toorish, Father Mulcahy and Guard Devenney breathed heavily in the passage. A silver pearl moved slowly down Guard Devenney's right cheek. The band of his uniform cap was soaked with sweat. He wiped the palms of his hands nervously on his trousers. Mrs Toorish screamed.

'Mother of God. Mother of God.'

She ran across the battlefield, disregarding the gun emplacements, the barbed wire, the redoubts. Soldiers, guns, horses were scattered by her best navy court shoes. She had taken care to dress herself suitably for her visit to the big house. She dragged at the arm of the still sleeping boy. He lay curled like a small animal in the warmth of the old man. The smell of whiskey grabbed at the woman's nose.

'Drink.'

She screamed again, only this time she didn't quite make it and only a sick whisper reached the ears of the men in the passage. The priest followed her into the room.

'Drunk. Drink everywhere. Oh, my God.'

The three men were silent, even their heavy breathing seemed to have stopped. The old man, totally confused as to what was going on, dream or reality, struggled painfully to sit up, to grasp the situation. The more he grasped, the more unpleasant the whole thing became. The mad woman, in an incongruous hat, dropped the boy's arm and began to hit Mr Prendergast in the face and chest with her soft, pink hands. It was like a nightmare. He hoped it was one. He dodged and struggled to get away from the damn woman, from her fists, from whatever dreadful, incomprehensible words were pumping from her mouth. As he moved he became conscious of the boy who had uncurled himself and was lying stretched on the floor, crying. His hands were clenched over his ears to keep out the sound of his mother's voice.

He put a hand down and touched him on the shoulder. 'There, there,' he whispered, like a mother to a child that had fallen in the road. He recognized the inadequacy of the words but was helpless.

'Take your dirty hands off my child.'

'He's frightened.'

'Frightened of his own mother, is it? Of you, more like, you dirty old . . .' She paused, even in her rage not liking to say the word with Father Mulcahy behind her in the doorway.

'He's confused. He was asleep. He doesn't understand what's going on yet. Give him a little time. Your behaviour is alarming.'

'I don't want to hear what you have to say.'

'I have very little to say. I'm not quite sure what you're doing in my house, uninvited.'

He had managed to get himself to his feet and was desperately searching for some rags of dignity to cover the humiliation that he was feeling. For the first time he became aware of the three men in the door. He bowed abruptly towards the priest, ignored Mr Toorish and addressed the guard.

'Ah, Guard Devenney, I take it you have a warrant. May I see it, please.' He held out his hand with all the authority of an officer and a gentleman. The guard fumbled in his pocket but merely pulled out a neatly folded handkerchief which he pushed up under the peak of his cap in an effort to stop the sweat running into his eyes.

'It's like this, sir . . .'

'The warrant.'

'Well you see . . .'

The priest spoke. 'Guard Devenney has no warrant. He's here at my request.'

'Information was laid . . .'

'Information was, as Devenney says, laid as to the whereabouts of the child.'

'If Guard Devenney has no warrant I would be pleased if he left my house at once. All of you with him. Have you never heard of the law of trespass?'

The priest turned a stern eye on the policeman, who was edging out into the passage. 'Stay where you are . . . Have you, Mr Prendergast, ever heard of what the law says about kidnappers?'

'I haven't kidnapped anyone.'

'I warn you that that may be the least of the charges against you, when all's said and done.'

'I think, Father, you're speaking out of turn.'

'We are all upset. I am here in support of this distracted woman.'

'I appreciate your position but I would be glad if you'd all leave the house. None of us can possibly think at this moment. Tomorrow morning at, say, eleven. Perhaps you would be good enough to come back then. We can discuss with clearer minds, perhaps . . .'

'There's nothing to discuss,' said Mr Toorish, speaking for the first time. 'We've nothing to discuss with you.'

The priest put a hand on his arm. 'I think . . .'

At this moment Mrs Toorish swooped like a hawk and dragged Diarmid to his feet. 'Has he hurt you, son? Has he touched you?'

The boy covered his face with his hands and continued to cry.

'He's drunk,' said Mrs Toorish with disgust, 'I can smell the drink on him.'

'My God, tonight,' muttered Mr Toorish. He picked at a loose thread on his coat. He, too, was dressed in his suit. The guard had faded from the room and could be heard shuffling his boots in the passage. This sort of affair tended to blow up in your face. He saw stormy interviews with the Super, maybe even the County Inspector, looming ahead. Invisible was the only thing to be.

'Come here to me, Diarmid.'

The priest spoke reasonably but the boy never moved. Father Mulcahy clicked his fingers with impatience. Mrs Toorish gave the boy a push towards the door.

'Didn't you hear Father Mulcahy . . . ?'

'Leave the child alone, can't you, woman. He's frightened and he's tired. Tomorrow morning we can . . .' Mr Prendergast touched the boy's shoulder as he stumbled past.

'Don't touch him,' screamed the mother.

The boy uncovered his eyes and looked around at the situation. The old man took a handkerchief from his pocket and handed it to him.

'Thanks.'

The priest took the boy by the shoulders and shook him gently. 'What have you to say for yourself, Diarmid Toorish, worrying the life out of your good mother like this?'

'Nothing, Father.'

'Not even "sorry, Father", hey?'

'No, Father.' He spoke the words so softly that only the priest could hear.

'Tch.' The fingers pressed warningly on the boy's shoulders.

'I'm not going home.' He looked up and stared the priest straight in the eye. 'I'm not going home. I mean it.'

Mrs Toorish began to cry. Dear God, dear boy, thought the old man, this is no time for heroics.

'So you're not. What do you intend to do with yourself, then, might I ask?'

The boy shook his head. 'I don't know.'

'You can't stay here, you know, and I'm sure you don't want to spend the night with Guard Devenney.'

'Is that a threat?' asked the old man angrily.

'My heart is broken,' sobbed the mother.

Guard Devenney, hearing his name mentioned, appeared like a ghost in the doorway, ready to vanish at a moment's notice.

'Let me handle things in my own way.'

'You're trying to intimidate the boy. Could he not spend what's left of the night, and God knows it's not much, with you?'

'When a man gets thrown from a horse, Mr Prendergast, you know as well as I he has to get straight back up again. It's better he goes tonight with them.'

'I'm not going home.' It was said this time with less conviction than before.

'You tell him,' suggested the priest.

'Off you go, Diarmid, with your mother. I'll see you in the morning.'

'You wouldn't make me.'

'Alas, boy, I have no alternative. No one will harm you. You have Father Mulcahy's word for that.'

'Yes,' said the priest. He looked around fiercely. 'No one will harm you.'

The group of them suddenly went quiet. Their faces were grey and exhausted, without energy or courage. They stood looking helplessly at each other. Outside, in the passage, the guard cleared his throat nervously.

The old man took his watch out of his pocket and looked at it, just for something to do. No one else seemed to know what to do or say next.

'Well. Yes. Eleven. How about eleven? We should be able to clear everything up then.'

The priest nodded. He pushed the boy before him out of the room. He said something to the guard that Mr Prendergast couldn't catch and then their feet started moving away, along the passage. Mr Toorish darted out of the room like a startled bird. He needed their protection.

'Fuck you, Mr Prendergast,' shouted Diarmid. His last heroic gesture. There was the sound of an almighty slap. Mr Prendergast closed his eyes. Mrs Toorish, who had remained standing in the centre of the room, made a sudden dash for the door, roughly pushing the old man to one side as she went.

'Wait. Don't leave me here with him.'

It was all over for the time being. The sound of steps disappeared, descended. In the distance Guard Devenney coughed. The hall door banged.

*   *   *

'Messing about,' said Alexander, 'forever messing about. You'll never get anywhere if you go on like that. Maybe the army'll teach you a thing or two.'

Mother laughed. The silver, beautiful laugh of a scornful girl.

'I shall go to my bed. It has been too long a day.'

'My bed, I believe, you sleep in these days . . .'

'Your bed, my dear Alexander, is six feet deep. Somewhere that is forever England.'

'Unkind.'

'I don't deny it. I have known little kindness in my life.'

'And practised less.'

The old man smiled sourly. 'I know my faults. I don't need to be judged by a . . .'

'Anyway,' interrupted his brother cheerfully, 'you've stuck your neck out now.'

'And you'll laugh when they cut my head off.'

'Dear Chas, it's nothing to what they did to me.'

'Water under the bridge.'

'Go to bed.' Alexander's voice was gentle. 'You'll know it all tomorrow.'

The old man felt the brush of a hand across his shoulder and then he was alone.

'I ought to be able to die.'

He never slept all night. The blackness of his room became grey and then blue. The chairs, book-littered tables, trousers, coats thrown with disregard here and there around the room turned from shadows into unhappy possessions. The birds, in the greyness, chattered to each other for a while and then were silent until the sun coloured the garden with golden early light and the grass was streaked with the long shadows of the moving trees. He lay on his back, tense with exhaustion. Sweat lay on his forehead like the beads of dew on the grass outside. His hands were clenched together as if he were praying.

A ludicrous situation that, in the end of all, the fag end of his life, he should be accused of being a sex maniac. There were almost elements of comedy in that. In his way of life passion had been an irrelevance, a trap for the uncautious man, creating unnecessary links between human beings. A form, to his way of thinking, of slavery. His desire for Clare, if it had ever existed, had been transitory. He had used her body from time to time as a means of relief rather than for the attainment of joy. After the conception of Sarah it had been finished. It was ludicrous. It must, at all costs, be kept from Sarah. It would blow over. Not soon enough. Perhaps it was a nightmare and he would wake up and find his disordered life was calm once more. To tangle with the Church, the Law and the local grocer all over the head of one small boy. Ludicrous was the only possible word. He repeated it several times aloud. The empty room was filled with the sound of the one word and he was reminded of the way Diarmid repeated words after him, planting them in his brain. 'What will they do with you now, little soldier?' He pushed the bedclothes aside and sat slowly around on the edge of the bed. His eyes were hot and encrusted. His heart pounded like an engine being driven too fast. Maybe he had a slight fever. At the very thought a rush of sweat burst out from under his soft hair and ran down the crevices of his face. He rubbed at his face with the back of one hand and groped for the cureall with the other. As the alcohol ran down his throat he felt more collected. He must shave, have a bath. The smell of his own sweat revolted him. Clean clothes. Put oneself into the right frame of mind for the coming interview. A suit, he thought as he stood up, is indicated. An old regimental tie, perhaps. The brave diagonal stripes covering a hollow man. If he could find it. Must be years. He made his way unsteadily to the bathroom.

*　*　*

He was at the piano playing Scarlatti when he heard the car arrive. He looked at his watch. Ten thirty. They were rushing him. He continued to play until the bell rang. Apart from his tie he made a poor figure. Since he had last worn this suit he seemed to have wasted and it hung around him as if he were a child dressed in his father's clothes. The sickness had left him now and he walked across the hall with what he hoped were the steps of a sane and confident man. It was neither the priest, the guard, nor the grocer on the step. It was the Rector.

'Oh,' said the old man, taken aback. 'Forgive me, James, but this is hardly the best moment . . .'

'Don't be ridiculous.' The Rector put a hand on his chest and pushed him back into the hall. He closed the door behind him. 'This is all most distasteful. I had to come. The place is alive with most horrible rumours. May we go into the study?'

'Of course.'

'I hardly know what to say.'

'Perhaps it would be best if you said nothing.'

'Why did you lie to me the other day? That angered me.'

'I evaded your questions. It really all seemed so pointless. What could you have done? I have been foolish, I admit that. Almost insane, I suppose.'

'Venal?'

The old man laughed. 'Of course not. I haven't evaded that question. I'm surprised you even asked it. You've known me a long time.'

'Acquaintances. As you have so often pointed out yourself.'

'Well enough to know the answer to that.'

'It's surprising the things you discover about people from time to time. Especially with regards to . . . eh . . . matters of an intimate nature.'

'Why have you come?'

'Duty . . . Eileen . . . as I said, I find it all most distasteful. There has never been . . .'

The old man held his hand up, like a policeman on point duty. 'No need to proceed.'

'If I felt I could help in any way, but . . .'

'Quite.'

'I . . . ah . . . would strongly advise you to go to England. On a visit. Extended. Right away, before they take any action.'

'Running away in the face of enemy fire, hey?'

'Whatever way you like to see it. I must look at it from the point of view of my congregation. There will be a scandal. It will be very unpleasant, very damaging for all concerned. Some good, ah, and well . . . People will be offended. If you disappear it may come to nothing. So many tales. People have short memories.'

'I have done nothing scandalous.'

'Who will believe that?'

'You?'

The Rector waved his hands distractedly.

'I don't really care one way or the other. I am distressed that the child should become embroiled in such unpleasantness. I shall do my best to straighten things out. This needs an element of good faith from the other side, though. If they possess such a thing.'

'Sarah, perhaps . . .'

'Absolutely no. I must insist, James, that under no circumstances . . .'

The Rector ran a nervous finger round the inside of his collar. 'If you really refuse all advice . . .'

'Certainly all that has been offered to date.'

'Then there's one last thing I'm afraid I must say . . .'

'Go ahead. We haven't much time.'

'I hope you won't take it amiss.'

'I'm sure, James, I will take it in the spirit in which it is given.'

'Until this . . . ah . . . yes . . . is all cleared up, I feel it would be best for all concerned if you allowed Eileen to take over your duties, vis à vis the choir. It might become an embarrassment to you.'

'Ah, yes. Of course.'

'I must think of my parishioners. If it was purely a personal matter, believe me. I have my duty.'

'Get on home, Rector. You've done your dreadful duty. Your God will forgive you. Do go home now, there's a good man, and leave me in peace. I have nothing more to say to you.'

He crossed the room slowly and stood at the window with his shrunken back towards the Rector.

'Ever.'

The Rector stood for a moment and watched while the old man pulled a flask out of his pocket, unscrewed the top and put it to his mouth. The man is mad, was written on his judging face. He shrugged slightly. Eileen was going to be very upset about all this. He tried to think of something appropriate to say, decided against it and left the house as quickly as he could.

The room was quite still. Mother would never have tolerated a situation of this kind. No one knew better how to keep them in their place. Mother would never have changed with the changing times and all, bar a few of them, would have bowed before her arrogance.

'Mother,' he implored, tucking the flask back into his pocket. But she had never come before. He wondered, irrelevantly, what

Sarah had done with her rings. He had been offended by her casual acceptance of them, by the way she had thrown them into the bottom of her bag. The garden looked neglected. The grass had not been cut since Sean left and a fine summer growth of weeds was starting to crowd the rose beds. Money was the only thing these people understood. He could make a good offer. Things could be sold. If not stocks, objects. The house was full of unwanted objects of no little value. After all, what would Sarah care? She had more than enough for one. And those rings, unused in the bottom of a drawer, no doubt. She had her mother's hands, practical hands, without distinction. What do I care about her, anyway? I gave her life. An established place among the more serious middle classes. He remembered the proprietorial pride suddenly with which he had read the telegram she had sent them on receiving the news of her double first. For some reason he hadn't even tried to explain to himself, he had pushed the telegram into his pocket and omitted to tell the news to Clare for several days. He had groped in his pocket at lunchtime and brought out the folded paper. He unfolded it and placed it on the table by his knives. It must have been about this time of year. The windows were open in the dining room and the buff paper stirred under his fingers. He had tried to smooth the creases out, erasing the evidence of delay, but then realized the foolishness of that and pushed the telegram across the table towards Clare, who was peeling ringlets of apple skin on to her plate. She waited until the apple was bare before picking up the paper. She had stared at it for a moment and then handed it back to him.

'I haven't got my glasses.'

He took the telegram, folded it once more and put it back in his pocket. 'It's merely from Sarah to say she's got a double first.'

Clare didn't say anything. She sliced through her apple, with a small silver knife. He had never been able to understand why she didn't eat an apple in her fingers like most other people in the world instead of treating it with the irritating reverence only due to more exotic fruit.

'A most admirable academic achievement.'

'You said merely.'

'Just a manner of speaking. Telegrams can be so final.'

'I'm delighted,' said Clare formally, as if she was uninvolved. 'Mother would have been so pleased.'

He didn't bother replying.

'Wouldn't she?' Her voice was plaintive.

'I beg your pardon?'

'Mother. So pleased?'

'I never could stand your mother. Damn Bloomsbury female.'

During the long pause that followed, Clare cut her apple up into even smaller pieces.

'I suppose it means she'll have no difficulty in getting a good job.'

'No problems at all. All sorts of doors open to her.'

'She won't have to rely on getting married, then.'

He reached across to the fruit bowl and took an apple. Shining red and green, one of the early crop from the orchard, with a sweet fresh smell. He bit into it angrily with his perfect teeth.

The clock on the mantelpiece struck eleven. He clasped his hands in front of him, rather as the Rector might have done, and turned away from the window. Pulses beat in all sorts of strange places in his body. As he turned, the door opened and Father Mulcahy came into the room followed by shadowy Mr

Toorish ducking his head this way and that, adding up things and translating them into money. Courage, thought the old man, do not leave me now.

'Your door was on the latch,' said the priest, 'so we took the liberty.'

'Good morning. Your punctuality is scrupulous.'

Mr Toorish muttered something incomprehensible.

'Won't you sit down.'

The three men sat down and stared at each other for a moment.

Mr Prendergast cleared his throat. 'Well, let's get down to discussion.'

The priest spoke sadly. 'I'm afraid there's nothing to discuss. We probably, in fact, shouldn't be here. But we had agreed . . . The boy has made a statement. To the guards.'

'Yer.' Mr Toorish fidgeted as he spoke with some coins in his pocket. Ill-gotten, no doubt, from the till, thought the old man. But, in spite of wry thoughts, panic was creeping in.

'He's confessed. Yer. It's all written down. In black and white.'

'Confessed?'

'That was what I said.'

The old man gave a disbelieving laugh. 'I'd be interested to know to what crime he has confessed.'

'He's confessed everything. He signed a statement at the barracks last night. The guards'll be on their way to take you in soon.'

'But . . .'

'That'll be enough, Toorish,' said the priest.

The old man put his hand to his head and looked at them in amazement. 'I really don't know what you're talking about. You gave me your word . . .'

'In good faith. It never occurred to me . . . What can you do?'

'Have you seen the statement?'

The priest nodded. 'I went to the barracks on my way here. It's . . . well . . . fairly damning.'

'Oh.'

'He has admitted to being under your influence. He has admitted to accepting presents from you, mitching from school at your request, drinking alcohol here in this house with you. Running . . . ah, naked in front of you, letting you touch him . . .'

'In particular places.'

'Toorish, please. You encouraged him to leave his parents and then locked him in the room upstairs . . .'

'I don't want to hear any more. You realize, don't you, that this is the most fantastic distortion.'

'You used him for your own corrupt purposes.'

'What utter rubbish. The boy wouldn't even know what you were talking about.'

'He signed it all. In the barracks. Only a few hours ago. They'll . . .'

'Toorish.'

He began to rattle the coins again. 'He says my son's a liar.'

'You know as well as I do that your son is not exactly an angel.'

'I had hoped that I might be able to do something for the boy.'

'Yer, and we all know what that was.'

'Toorish.'

'Sorry, Father.'

'I would just like, if you'd bear with me for a few minutes, to put things in perspective.' He looked anxiously at the priest.

'Go ahead.'

'I . . .'

'Hold your tongue, Toorish.'

Mr Toorish continued to jingle the coins, if not to speak. His face was fatigued and mean but there was a distinct air of triumph about him that someone else other than himself was on the receiving end of trouble. This would take the wife's mind off the petty cash all right.

'My version. You may believe it to be distortion if you like, but I should like you to hear it. The boy came here first with a message from his mother. Something about working in the garden, if I remember aright. Isn't that so, Toorish?'

Mr Toorish moved his head uneasily but didn't say anything. He wasn't going to commit himself. The coins were silent in his pocket.

'He seemed genuinely interested in me and my belongings. Totally uninterested in school. A bit of an original, I thought. He took to coming up here to visit me. I admit to being at fault here. I suppose I should have sent him away with a flea in his ear. I didn't. That's the crux, really. He came to talk, listen, read, just be about. I admit I enjoyed his company. I suppose I must have been lonely without, so to speak, realizing. Hardly a crime.'

He got up, unable to sit under their watching eyes any longer. He walked over to the window. Mother would have disposed of them long since. She would have rung the bell for Helen Peoples, the parlour-maid, to come and show them out.

'Well . . .' began the priest uncertainly.

'He didn't want to be a grocer. Apart from anything else, it didn't appeal to him as a way of life. I'm not expressing myself very well, I'm afraid. You must appreciate . . .'

'Yes, yes.' The priest looked apprehensively at Mr Toorish out of the side of his eye.

'He came up to ask me would I give him enough money to go to England. I told him to go home and talk to his parents, that running away at his age would get him nowhere. Something on those lines, anyway.'

The jingling started again.

'Would you stop.' Father Mulcahy turned angrily on his companion who pulled his hand out of his pocket as if he'd been hit.

'Quite,' muttered the old man. 'I told him to go home. I wanted neither part nor parcel of his problems. I assure you, at that moment I was prepared to wash my hands of the child.'

He made a feeble handwashing gesture. This is ridiculous. I am justifying myself. I am whining. I am frightened.

'He came back without my knowing. Established himself. What could I do. I was his friend.'

'He has signed a statement. Isn't that enough for you? What are we listening to this for?'

'I presume the law knows as well as I, you, Toorish, and I . . . how easy it is to obtain statements from frightened people.'

Father Mulcahy sighed. 'There are very unpleasant implications in that remark.'

'I am not a perverted man.'

'There is also a witness.'

Mother and Alexander crossed the lawn on the way to the tennis court. She had her arm through his and smiled up into his face. It was the day before . . . They had drunk champagne by the tennis court and late that night they had swum in the lake. It had been full of stars which lay, he remembered, in his cupped hands, like the bubbles in the champagne glasses.

'A witness?'

Mr Toorish began to laugh.

'How can you have a damn witness?'

'You see, me bucko, we have you where we want you. There was Sean Brady watching every move you made and you never knew. He saw your mauling and your conniving and not ashamed to tell either.'

'Enough, enough,' said the priest wearily.

'You really are amazing.' He put a hand against the wall to steady himself. The world was spinning.

'Not a bit afraid of those that might think they were his betters.'

The priest put out a hand and touched Mr Toorish gently on the arm. 'Please.'

Mr Toorish shrugged the hand off ungraciously. 'There's no reason to stay. He's got the picture now.' He stood up.

'There's just one thing I'd like to know before you go. The boy? What will happen to him?'

'You'd like to know, wouldn't you?'

'I thought it was best if he left here as soon as possible . . .'

'There's no need to speak a word, Father.'

'I'm not too sure that this man is the kind of devil you're making him out to be.'

'Isn't there the statement? Don't you tell me a kid could make up that sort of thing.'

'With judicious questions . . . who knows . . . In this country, thank God, every man is innocent until it's proved otherwise.'

'About the boy . . .'

'I have arranged for him to go to the Christian Brothers in

Cork. They will take good care of him for a year or two. From now on, late though it be, I shall take a concerned interest in his welfare. I feel, Mr Prendergast, that I, too, have been lax in my duties.'

'I couldn't see him before he goes?'

'I'm afraid that's out of the question.'

'He has made a very serious accusation behind my back. I would like him to make it, if he will, to my face.'

'That will be for the law to decide. In time. He's leaving here this afternoon. I shall take him to Cork myself and see him bestowed.'

'That's something, anyway.'

They looked at each other with a glimmer of understanding. 'Hmm.'

The priest stood up slowly. 'I used to be a bit of a pianist myself once.'

'Indeed.'

'When I was a curate. My duties then were not so time-consuming and, I suppose, I had the energy of youth. I must confess I sometimes stop and listen when you're playing the organ. Thank God, anyway, for Bach.'

'Amen. I don't play like I used to. My fingers are stiff these days.'

'Old age comes to us all. I've often wished we had an organist like yourself. Owen Doherty is hardly an artist. Mind you, that's just between these four walls.' He paused. They had both forgotten Mr Toorish whose mean eyes shifted from one to the other, like someone watching a tennis match. 'Perhaps, when all this has blown over, we might, ah, look out some duets. What with your stiffness and my lack of practice we might be well matched.'

'Do you honestly think, Father, that all this will blow over?'

The priest thought for a moment. 'No. I don't suppose it will. Their blood is up. Were you ever a hunting man?'

'My brother.'

'Ah, yes. Before my time. I heard of him, though. A great man, by all accounts. There's this . . . well, it's hard to put into words . . . feeling of excitement that sometimes happens. Closeness. To the humans and animals alike. A sudden single-mindedness. No obstacle is too great. Their corporate mind is on one thing, the kill. And when that happens, God help the fox.'

'You don't sound as if you liked your flock, or should I say pack, very much, Father.'

'I understand them. I try to love them. I have very few illusions about the human breed, Mr Prendergast, or about my own inadequacies as a guide. But I do try to love them. I find there's very little more I can do . . . I've wished many times that you had been one of mine. The thought has often been in my mind that I could have helped you.'

'Maybe I didn't need your help.'

'We all need help. There has never yet been a human being that didn't.'

The old man went over to the glass case. He opened it and stood for a while looking at the contents. He picked up the medals first and then, after a moment's hesitation, the four miniatures. Only dark patterns lay on the velvet when he closed the case again. 'Here.' He held them out to the priest. 'Give these to the boy. He's the only one has any interest any more. This one is reputed to be by Teniers.' He held up a smiling young man. 'He might get some money for it in years to come.'

The priest hesitated to take them.

'What's that?' Mr Toorish came to life at the sound of the word 'money'. He moved towards the two older men, his hand groping in his pocket once more for the comfort of the coins. 'What's that?'

The priest accepted the offering into his hands. 'This one, you say?'

'Yes. I'd say a couple of hundred. Who knows. It might come in useful sometime.'

'I'll see he gets them.'

'Money,' squealed Mr Toorish. 'Is money changing hands?'

'A handful of military medals.' Father Mulcahy waved them in front of his eyes.

'There's no use trying to buy me off. The whole thing's in the hands of the law.'

'Don't worry,' said the priest. 'Leave it all to me.' He stowed the medals away in his pockets and then the miniatures. He pulled a large white handkerchief from his breast pocket and carefully wrapped it round the possible Teniers.

'Thank you.'

'I insist on being told what's going on.' He rattled the coins savagely.

'He was interested in those medals. That's all. I thought he might like to have them.'

'I don't know that it's right. My wife . . .'

'You can discuss it later with Father Mulcahy. Now, if you'll excuse me . . . I think there's little left to say . . . I don't feel quite myself . . . I would be grateful if you'd go.'

The priest put out a hand to touch him and thought the better of it. 'Have you no friend would come? I myself would call . . .' Mr Prendergast didn't seem to hear. '. . . Could see you through?'

'I will be all right, thank you. You have been kinder than might have been expected.'

'I'd say the guards will be here quite soon.'

'They've asked me to stop playing the organ in the church.'

'I understand that.'

'You seem to understand a lot.' His voice was cold.

'Without understanding there is no forgiveness. Without forgiveness there is no grace.'

'Bah.'

'You have a hard road in front of you, my friend. I shall pray for you.'

'Thank you.'

The priest turned to go, pushing Mr Toorish in front of him across the room. As they reached the door the old man spoke again.

'I loved the boy. Do love. Yes.'

'There's an admission for you. Did you hear that, Father? Out of his own mouth.' He looked at the priest with admiration in his eyes. 'Didn't you work him up to that well. I thought you were reneging on us with all those soft words but, by God, you were working him up. We have him for certain sure.'

'In the name of God . . .' Father Mulcahy raised his fist as he shouted and it looked as if he was going to hit the man as he had hit his son the night before. He let his arm fall to his side and laughed, embarrassed. 'May God forgive me. You see, I too, have my problems. Thank you for saying that, my friend.'

'Oh, do go away,' muttered the old man. He needed a drink desperately but didn't like to produce the flask in their presence.

'Yes.'

The two men left the room. Mr Prendergast lowered himself into his chair by the window. He waited until he heard their voices in the garden and then he pulled the flask from his pocket and drank deeply from it. He lay back in his chair and the late summer sun shone full in his face. He closed his eyes, which otherwise watered in the brilliance of the golden light. He only moved to raise the bottle to his lips from time to time and lower it again. He was still there four hours later. The sun had dropped behind the trees and its rays now gilded the ceiling. Dust danced lazily in the golden light. No squad car had arrived. No guard with notebook and ballpoint pen. No Alexander, no mother, not even Clare. No one disturbed his peace. A wasp crawled slowly across the window. Maybe the priest and that terrible little grocer had been creations of his tired mind. Last night also. How long could it all go on for? He must have some rest. Peace. Darkness, so that he could open his eyes without the pain that seemed to be splitting his head in half. He made his way over to the piano. Books of music were in piles all over the top. Some fell on the floor as he searched. Eventually he found Chopin's Nocturnes. He began to play. He felt as if he had never played like this before. The music came leaping out from under his fingers and filled the world.

* * *

The two guards heard the sound of the piano as they came round the last corner before the house.

'He's there, anyway,' remarked Guard Conroy.

'True enough.'

'He's a great hand on the piano.'

'I thought yeez were never coming.'

Sean stepped out from behind a rhododendron bush. He was looking very old and very mad. He peered up at them both from under the brim of his cap. Devenney put a foot on the ground.

'What are you doing hanging around here, anyway?'

'I've been here all day, waiting to see he doesn't get away on you.'

'If we need your help we'll ask for it. Get away off now and don't be hanging around here.'

'Have it your own way. He could a got into the car and driven away all the time you've been coming.'

Guard Conroy circled round and came back to see what was going on. 'Trouble?'

'There's always trouble with him around.'

Sean backed away from them into the bushes once more. The two guards looked at each other and shrugged.

'He's been banging on that piano for near on an hour now. As if he didn't care. That'll show you the bad is in him.' Sean's voice came out of the bushes.

'If you don't get out of here double quick,' said Guard Devenney, pushing off with his foot, 'I'll have you inside for trespass.'

The hall door was wide open. They knocked, as a formality, but didn't wait for an answer. They walked across the hall towards the music. The old man never heard them come into the room. They both stood in silence, listening. The younger man glanced at the other with embarrassment.

'Mr Prendergast.' His voice made no impression. 'If you'll excuse me, Mr Prendergast.'

The old man took his hands off the keys. His head was shaking gently back and forth. He turned round to face the two guards.

'That was as near perfection as I will ever achieve. Ever have ... ever.' He peered at them, screwing his eyes up to thin lines. 'I presume you exist. I think I have been waiting for you. Yes.' He suddenly looked slightly puzzled and his hands went to his side.

The older guard spoke. 'If you wouldn't mind coming down to the barracks, sir, there's a couple of questions . . .'

'By all means. Clear things . . .'

He stood up, painfully, slowly, his hand still on his side. His fingers almost clutching.

'Indigestion.'

'We can wait till it passes, sir. There's no need to rush yourself.'

'Sit down again. A minute or two.'

Guard Conroy was alarmed by the way the old fellow's face seemed to be collapsing in front of his very eyes.

'Can I get you something?'

The old man shook his head. But the effort to do even that was too much.

'Ah . . .'

The two guards rushed to him. He gestured to them to keep their distance.

'Leave me.'

He fell. His shoulders shuddered for a few moments and that was all.

'Oh, my God,' said Guard Devenney. He took off his cap. Conroy bent down and touched the old man's body.

'He's gone all right.' He took his cap off, too; then, not quite knowing what to do with it, he put it on again.

'You'd better ring the barracks and the doctor, I suppose. Yes.'

As he spoke, Devenney took his notebook out of his pocket. He looked at his watch and began to write. After a moment he realized that Conroy was still fidgeting in the doorway.

'Well, get on, can't you?'

'The telephone . . . ?'

'Search for it, man. If you can't find a telephone in an empty house you're not fit to be in the force.'

Conroy left the room. Guard Devenney finished what he had to write and put the notebook back in his pocket. He looked down at Mr Prendergast.

'Well, I don't know . . . I just don't know. You poor bloody old sod, you've saved us a pile of trouble, anyway.'

You can buy any of these other **Review** titles from your bookshop or *direct from the publisher*.

FREE P&P AND UK DELIVERY
(Overseas and Ireland £3.50 per book)

Sitting Practice	Caroline Adderson	£6.99
Ghost Music	Candida Clark	£6.99
Intuition	Peter Jinks	£6.99
This is Not a Novel	Jennifer Johnston	£6.99
The Song of Names	Norman Lebrecht	£6.99
Nightdancing	Elizabeth Garner	£6.99
The Secret Life of Bees	Sue Monk Kidd	£6.99
My Lover's Lover	Maggie O'Farrell	£6.99
Blue Noon	Robert Ryan	£6.99
Revenge	Mary Stanley	£6.99
The Hound in the Left-Hand Corner	Giles Waterfield	£6.99
The Woman Who Painted Her Dreams	Isla Dewar	£6.99

TO ORDER SIMPLY CALL THIS NUMBER

01235 400 414

or visit our website: www.madaboutbooks.com

Prices and availability subject to change without notice.